I0586222

TOGETHER

A SPIRITUAL FICTION SERIES

WALDMEER SERIES
BOOK 2

DONNA GODDARD

Copyright © 2017, 2023

All rights reserved.

No part of this book may be reproduced, stored in a retrieval system, or transmitted in any form or by any means — electronic, mechanical, photocopying, recording, or otherwise — without prior written permission from the author, except for brief quotations used in reviews.

Second Edition 2023

Published by Donna Goddard

Victoria, Australia

Paperback ISBN: 978-0645729610

Large Print ISBN: 978-0645875508

Cover design by Donna Goddard

www.donnagoddard.com

CONTENTS

PART I
TOGETHER IN WALDMEER

ALAMGIR

CHAPTER 1
CONQUEROR OF THE WORLD

Amira hadn't had the nightmare since she was twenty. Back then, she was known as Maria. The nightmare hadn't crossed her mind during the two years she had been living in Eraldus. Now that she was travelling back to Waldmeer each weekend, it was occasionally returning.

That was strange because nothing could be more charming than Waldmeer—going to sleep to the distant sea, waking to forest birds, walking to the rhythm of the breaking waves.

Some years ago, Maria came face to face with the malevolent nightmare when she went to see her teacher, Erdo, in the forest. That was the first time Amira spoke to her, and the beginning of many years of instruction.

Now, Maria was back in the Homeland, and Amira had sole charge of the body they had shared. Some years had been lost in the transition, and Amira was in her late thirties, though she seemed somewhat ageless.

"Erdo, is that you? What are you doing here?" said Amira when coming out of the Waldmeer Post Office.

There before her was a smiling Erdo. He was dressed like one of the local dairy farmers, complete with muddy boots and felt hat. She had not seen him since her weekly return to Waldmeer, although she thought she saw someone who looked like him a few times. It dawned on her that it must have been Erdo all along.

She recalled that he looked like a forty-year-old businessman with an Armani suit and slicked-back hair last week. Another time, he looked like a retired city dweller visiting his holiday house, with less hair and plumper than the previous sleek version. Yet, it was the same unmistakable Erdo expression—a cross between amusement, exasperation, and compassion.

"I have come to see you," said Erdo.

That's a privilege, thought Amira. *Erdo rarely leaves the forest. His students go to him.*

"Let's walk," said Erdo. "Do you remember before your twenty-first birthday, you met Alamgir?"

"Alamgir?" asked Amira, recalling no one of that name.

"Yes, Alamgir," said Erdo, "the darkness from your nightmare that day in the Leleks."

"Oh, is that its name," said Amira.

"Yes, it means *conqueror of the world,*" said Erdo.

"I hope it isn't," said Amira, pulling a face.

"No, but it tries," said Erdo. "It takes every opportunity it can. The few years you have been away from Waldmeer in Eraldus, it has been winning quite a bit."

"Can't you stop it?" said Amira.

"I am not allowed," said Erdo. "The Advisors of the Homeland forbid interference with human choices. It is how humans learn. They must sleep in the bed they make until they make a different one."

"I see," said Amira.

"One day, everyone will realise that they don't even need a bed," laughed Erdo, "because sleep is a respite from a tiresome world made up of the problems created in the day."

Come to think of it, Amira had never seen Erdo's bed and, for that matter, never seen his house. He had always just appeared in the forest after she crossed the old walking bridge next to the peaceful pond with the black swans. She looked up at him to ask about his house, but he was gone.

CHAPTER 2
DEMOLITION

T homas was tearing out pages from the local Waldmeer paper to use as kindling for his fireplace. He glanced at one of the pages and saw a small advertisement.

Healer available in Waldmeer on weekends. Call Amira.

The address given was Lucy and Lenny's old house.

Maria must have changed her name to Amira after her parents died, thought Thomas. *I guess Amira is a more exotic name than Maria for a healer.*

He imagined a crystal ball and heavy, closed curtains. Healers were not exactly his style, but for some reason, he stuck the ad on his fridge. That morning, Thomas had stopped his car at the end of his street outside Kathleen's house. The bulldozers were there. The house was already half demolished. He sat transfixed as if the machine was methodically ripping out pieces of him with each assault on the house. He couldn't bear to watch it, nor could he drive away.

"You better hurry up, Mr MacArthur, or you'll be late for your own staff meeting," yelled one of his young teachers as he drove past on the way to Waldmeer State Secondary School. "I can run it if you like."

Thomas waved him on with a forced laugh and started his engine again. He knew by the time he drove home, the last trace of Kathleen would have vanished. It was painful. He didn't want to go to school. He didn't want to go home. He just wanted to crawl up in a little ball and die. How could he have let this happen? He didn't even know how it happened.

CHAPTER 3
KATHLEEN

T all and slim, with shoulder-length, slightly curly hair, Kathleen was always beautifully groomed, although she never looked *groomed*. She just looked beautiful, as if she had woken up like that. Possibly, she did because she rarely wore makeup. She had more than a touch of the wild woman in her. She was never happier than on the beach with the wind wreaking havoc with her curly locks. She didn't hide from the sun, so her face had a healthy glow. She was willing to accommodate the lines in return for the benefits of being outside. Anyway, she owned her lines. They added to her appeal as if to say, *Don't mess with me. I'm no insecure young kitten.*

Kathleen's husband was a prominent doctor in the city. He had an extensive career, and part of his work was with the underprivileged. Although Kathleen had spent most of her time raising children, running a busy home, and supporting her husband, she was no second fiddle. Accomplished in her own career before children, she was a constant source of wise advice to her husband and contributed greatly to his professional success. They had more than enough money for their needs, but refused to live in one of the city's wealthy suburbs. They did, however, allow themselves the luxury of a holiday house in Waldmeer. They bought it more than twenty years ago. It was a few houses away from Thomas and his wife.

Kathleen and her husband did not enjoy the company of Thomas's wife. She was the opposite of Kathleen. Short, fine-boned, and fragile. She complained about the sun and equally complained about the cold. She always seemed ill in some way, if not physically, then emotionally. Whereas Kathleen's attractiveness seemed to grow with age, the years were not kind to Thomas's wife. Perhaps she was not kind to the years. In retrospect, she even seemed old when they all first met and were less than forty.

Thomas's wife often remarked, "Marriage is for life. These days, people seem to have no loyalty or perseverance."

Kathleen thought, *People who have the most to gain out of a relationship are the ones who say, "Marriage is for life, no matter what." They say it as if they are so virtuous when, really, they are warning their partner that if they leave, they will be held accountable.*

It was enough to keep a man like Thomas in check. Thomas worried about what many people thought, not just his wife. There was no question of leaving.

As tedious as it was to tolerate Thomas's wife, it was easy to love Thomas. He was their first friend in Waldmeer, ensuring all the other locals accepted and welcomed them. He kept an eye on their house when they were in the city. He was a genuine and good person devoted to his school and community. Thomas couldn't help but secretly fall in love with Kathleen. He probably fell for her the first time they met, but he wouldn't allow himself such thoughts. Besides, he was as much in awe of her marriage as he was of her. It was so honest and productive. Kathleen and her husband were true friends and survived the ups and downs of life and marriage with the grace of two well-balanced, focused, and altogether lovely people.

Thomas's wife often seemed on the verge of a life-and-death sickness. Eventually, she got one that killed her. Several years later, Kathleen's husband, who had rarely been ill, died from an unforeseen medical issue. It was only natural for Thomas and Kathleen to continue their friendship.

CHAPTER 4
SHORT SKIRTS

"You are punching above your weight," joked a friend to Thomas as he and Kathleen walked into the restaurant for dinner.

Thomas knew he was. He was so thrilled to be in a relationship with Kathleen. When Thomas first asked Kathleen, she was hesitant, but seeing his need, she accepted.

Although Thomas was thrilled about the relationship, almost no one else in Waldmeer was. They were used to him being with an ineffectual person, not someone with Kathleen's dignity and intelligence. It seemed to them they had much to lose and little to gain.

Alamgir whispered into their ears, and they heeded him. They could not hear the other voice—that Kathleen had their best interest at heart.

The first outright enemy was a young teacher at school with short skirts but big ambitions. She was an attractive woman in her early thirties—highly manipulative, with Thomas easily wrapped around her finger.

Over a few years, she had wooed, flirted, and seduced

her way into the top spot of his favourites. Although Thomas told himself she was a great asset to the school, everyone could see he had been hoodwinked.

Of course, Kathleen realised this instantly and tried to help Thomas rectify the situation by putting the girl back in her rightful place. The girl's eyes were glued on the prize of easy power, and she would have none of it. Thomas, she could handle. Kathleen, she could not. Kathleen had to go. It was a matter of survival.

The young teacher lied her way through the teachers, school administrators, and townsfolk. Her malice matched her ambition. People knew she was a liar, but they were intimidated by Kathleen and preferred the girl's seductive foolishness to Kathleen's self-assurance and courage.

Alamgir was delighted with the choice.

The school and townsfolk refused to invite Kathleen to events as Thomas's partner, even though everyone else was invited. Thomas said nothing. They would walk past, paying their respects to him and giving Kathleen a sour smile, if anything at all. Thomas said nothing. He should have fired the girl, but he wouldn't. He did nothing.

In the end, it was the girl who held all the firepower.

CHAPTER 5
FIRE

One evening, Thomas couldn't sleep. He was sitting on his balcony listening to the night sounds, wondering what to do about the situation with Kathleen, which had been escalating. Just as he got up to go back to bed and wrestle with sleep, he looked over to her house. He could see the furthest point of her back garden from his balcony. He was startled to see a flame.

Maybe it's a light flickering, he thought.

It wasn't. It was a fire, and it was rapidly gaining momentum.

Oh no, Kathleen's back shed is on fire, he thought.

He ran barefoot up the street to her house while dialling the fire brigade.

"Kathleen, wake up. There's a fire in your backyard," yelled Thomas as he banged on her front door.

The Waldmeer Fire Department didn't often have emergencies. In a relatively short time (for a department unused to emergencies), they were there with hoses and extinguished the fire.

"I'm sorry, Kathleen," said the head of the department, "but this was no accident. Someone poured petrol on your shed and lit it deliberately."

Kathleen and Thomas knew who it was. The girl had many young male fans in Waldmeer, any number of whom could have carried out a favour in the hope of a return one.

That was the end for Kathleen. She knew that to continue would end in her own destruction. Thomas either couldn't or wouldn't stop it. She told herself that he couldn't, but somewhere in her heart, she wondered if it was that he wouldn't. The next morning, she went to the real estate agent and asked him to put her treasured holiday home up for sale.

"I think it's for the best," said the real estate agent in a kind, resigned manner. "You have a wonderful life in the city. You don't need us. It is we who could have benefited from you."

In the end, few were Kathleen's friends—few, indeed.

The young teacher remained at Waldmeer Secondary School. Thomas told himself that it was best to keep the peace and not cause any more trouble.

Alamgir laughed.

CHAPTER 6
CONQUEROR OF NOTHING

Kathleen's brother was a Zen Buddhist monk. He lived in the hills, outside the city, and helped run a retreat centre. Now that Kathleen no longer had a house in Waldmeer, she visited him weekly to have contact with nature and solitude. His monk name was Aishi, meaning *compassionate service.* He was true to his name.

"They were so damn mean," said Kathleen to her brother as they walked along the winding path of the hermitage.

After listening for some time, Aishi asked, "What is it that you want? An apology?"

"Apologies are cheap,' said Kathleen.

"What is it then?" asked Aishi.

Kathleen stopped walking and looked at her brother. "It's Thomas," she said. "I want to know I didn't waste the last few years of my life."

Aishi smiled. He had the serenity of one who lives as part of nature's ongoing, never-failing transformations.

THAT EVENING, in Waldmeer, Thomas stared at the ad on his fridge.

Healer available in Waldmeer on weekends. Call Amira.

It had been a gruelling day after watching the demolition of Kathleen's house.

It's worth a try, he thought, not knowing what else to do.

A few days later, in Amira's lounge room, Thomas said rather awkwardly, "I suppose you have heard about Kathleen and me."

"We are a small town," said Amira.

"Don't believe everything you hear," said Thomas.

His words rang hollow.

"I don't believe everything I hear," said Amira in a tone that surprised Thomas. "She was a gift to you. I hope you looked after her."

"Of course I did," said Thomas, unsure of the direction this was going.

He attempted to tell the story in more detail. Amira was silent.

Eventually, he blurted out, "I just want her back."

"Kathleen is not coming back," said Amira. "Why would she? You were willing to take everything she had, which was a lot, and then let the wolves eat her so long as they didn't eat you."

Thomas was shocked by Amira's bluntness and what she was implying.

"Are you suggesting I wanted to hurt her?" he said.

"I am saying that you wanted to use her for your advantage without paying the price," said Amira.

"What sort of person would do that?" said Thomas, not waiting for the answer.

He stood up to leave.

"Thank you for your assistance, but I won't be requiring your services anymore," he said as if firing an out-of-line employee.

Amira knew she was being tough on him, but she had to be. This was his chance. Otherwise, he would slip into the next few decades with decline and loneliness as his companions.

Thomas gave Amira her money and abruptly left.

TWO WEEKS LATER, he was back.

"I have been through every emotion," he said wearily. "Mostly anger. I was angry that you implied I could be so selfish and gutless."

Amira remained quiet as she was not sure where he was up to in his healing.

"It took me a week to stop being furious with you," said Thomas. "Then I started to feel terribly sad and, worse than that, guilty. I still feel overwhelmed with guilt, and I will probably never be able to get rid of it."

"Don't get bogged down in the guilt," said Amira. "It is as egotistical as the anger. The ego is fragile and brutal, and no one is safe from its betrayals. It will always choose what it thinks is in its best interest, for the cheapest price. It may be as blatant as short skirts and lies, or hidden behind kind words—but it comes from the same place: using people to get what we want, or trying to remove those who stand in our way."

"I don't have anything else but school and Waldmeer," said Thomas by way of explanation. "The last thing I wanted to do was hurt Kathleen, but I can't afford to lose the only thing I have."

"If that were true, then your choice would be understandable," said Amira. "However, what you are holding onto is quite worthless. You must already suspect this, or you would not have come to me and certainly would not have returned after the first bruising visit."

They both laughed.

"Although Kathleen was a gift to you," said Amira, "learning this is a greater gift."

As Amira waved to Thomas from the front gate, she looked down to the beach at the bottom of the street. The sunlight was playing on the water.

"You are not conqueror of the world, Alamgir," said Amira. "You are conqueror of nothing."

BUNGALOW BUDDIES

CHAPTER 7
TRANSLUCENT MAN

The past few weekends in Waldmeer, Amira had been seeing a man out of the corner of her eye. She could tell the man was no longer an Earth resident because he was translucent. That made it easy!

He was about her age. Tall, blonde, broad shoulders like a footballer. Amira felt that it was not her that he wanted to speak to. She guessed he wanted to communicate with someone in Waldmeer who couldn't see him. She had no idea who, but life always has a way of telling us what we need to know.

IDE LOOKED at his sleeping body. She loved those strong, broad shoulders. It was not only a beautiful body, but so far, it had proved itself to be a resilient one after all that he had put it through. Fabian's body was not yet showing the ravages of recurring addiction.

He was probably more at home in his body than

anywhere else in this world. His mind was fractured. His spirit fragile. Yet, his body had always served him well. In sports, in love, he radiated physical health and competence.

She wished he would not destroy his beautiful body with a sick mind, but knew it was only a matter of time. After waking up, Ide realised she had been dreaming again. Fabian died eight months ago.

Not long after their baby was born, Fabian went to jail for a drug-related offence from his younger years. Ide lost him to prison for three years. When he returned, he was good for some years, but the addiction kicked in again. He was in and out of rehab.

He was killed in a car accident earlier this year. He was drunk. This time, she and her boy lost him permanently. No one said it, but many felt his death had freed Ide and her by now twelve-year-old boy to have a normal life.

Ide appreciated their concern, but they did not realise, and perhaps could not, that Fabian paid for Ide's love with his own. As broken as he was, he loved her.

Ide looked at the other Waldmeer women and rarely saw in their husbands' eyes the devotion she saw in Fabian's. That was worth a lot. There was no need for pity because Ide knew she had been loved.

CHAPTER 8
ENERGY FIELD

One Saturday afternoon, Ide made her way to the meeting she had been invited to. She didn't want to go. She was still grieving and didn't want to do anything, but she was told that the meeting organiser had a bright money-making proposal. Ide needed the money. Amira had also been invited. There were fifteen other people present.

When Amira walked into the room, she noticed a woman about her age with fair skin, calm blue eyes, delicate features, and a gentle energy field. She had occasionally seen the woman around Waldmeer but knew nothing about her.

"Hello, I'm Amira," she said, sitting beside the woman.

"I'm Ide," said the woman. "Nice to meet you."

"Ide? That's an Irish name. That explains your looks," said Amira, smiling.

"Welcome to the first meeting of the Bungalow Buddies," said a friendly, round woman in her early sixties. "As you are probably aware, seventeen of the houses in Waldmeer have an identical bungalow on their property. They originally came from the old hotel near the pier, where seasonal workers once stayed. When the hotel no longer needed them, the bungalows were offered to locals—provided they moved them themselves."

Amira remembered how her (Maria's) father had jumped at the opportunity and enlisted his fishing mates to haul the bungalow up the hill into their back garden. It still sat there twenty years later on rough blocks of tree trunks, the floor slightly uneven but workable.

"A few bungalows have gone to rack and ruin," the meeting convenor continued. "One or two have been updated and are now quite fancy. However, I understand that most of them are substantially unchanged and empty. I'm sure that together we can do something lovely and constructive with our bungalows."

The woman's inclusive, good-willed nature quickly won everyone over.

After a pleasant meeting, the convenor said, "We will meet again in a month. Good luck with fixing up your bungalows and finding tenants."

CHAPTER 9
BE THERE

Charlie and her partner, Mary, had been living in the share house in Eraldus for more than two years. Charlie had decided it was time to sell her property in the back hills of Waldmeer and buy a house in the city with Mary.

It was only a few years, but it felt like a lifetime (perhaps a different lifetime) since Amira had driven up the long, dirt driveway of Charlie's property in the back hills. She parked outside her old shed, which Charlie had affectionately named *Maria's Shrine*. She peeked in as she walked past. There was nothing in it except a few items on the windowsill. Farkas had been renting Charlie's property since his return from the North Country. Amira hadn't let Farkas know she was coming. She didn't have his number. Anyway, she felt it was best to catch him off guard. She took a deep breath and knocked on the door. Nothing. She was fairly sure that he already knew she was there. He had eyes like an eagle and a sixth sense to match. She decided that the best option was to wait patiently. That way, he would know that she was not kidding about wanting to talk to him. Somewhat resigned, he came to the door.

"Hello, Amira," said Farkas. "It's been a while since you have been in these parts."

"Yes, it has," said Amira.

Farkas didn't invite her in.

"I know it's none of my business...' said Amira.

That was a mistake. She immediately felt Farkas prickle.

"Charlie told me she is selling her property and already has a buyer who wants to live in it," said Amira. "Obviously, you will have to move soon."

"And?" said Farkas. "Your point?"

"I have a friend who lives a few streets from me," said Amira. "She is at the bottom of your old street."

"Go on," said Farkas.

He must need somewhere to move, or he wouldn't let me continue, thought Amira.

"I know it's not much," said Amira, "but she has a bungalow and needs someone to rent it. It's cheap."

"Why are you interested in me living there?" said Farkas, not one to beat around the bush. "I'm sure you are aware that I am quite capable of finding my own accommodation."

"Of course you are," said Amira, trying to soften him.

Farkas was unimpressed.

"Why?" he repeated.

Amira said honestly, "My friend is a lovely woman. She has a son who is twelve now. They have been through a lot. The husband had a problem with addiction. Not long after their boy was born, he went to jail. Later, he was in and out of rehab. Eight months ago, he was killed in a car accident. I know he brought it on himself, but he loved his wife and boy, and they loved him."

"Well, I'm sorry for them," said Farkas, "but I don't see what it has to do with me."

"I thought that if you lived there for a while," said Amira, "it might help them by having a man around the place. You wouldn't have to do anything. Just be there."

Amira paused and then said more bluntly, "Maybe care. That would help."

"Thanks for the suggestion," said Farkas, "but no thanks. I have enough of my own problems."

He put his hand on the doorknob to indicate it was time to go.

Amira didn't budge.

"Look, Farkas, it's not just them. It's you. Do you intend to be a hermit for the rest of your life? It's not good for you."

Farkas stared at Amira and spoke down to her, "I have told you before that my life is none of your business. What I do or don't do has nothing to do with you. I can't make this any clearer than I already have."

Not quite ready to concede defeat, Amira said with quiet determination, "You are not the only one suffering. Don't you think you could reach out to someone else and help a bit? You might even find it gives your life some meaning."

Time to go, thought Amira.

She didn't bother saying goodbye. The time for niceties seemed to have been over a few moments ago, probably after the first sentence.

CHAPTER 10
DONE DEAL

"Hi, Gabriel," said Amira, answering her phone. "How are you?"

"Hi Maria," said Gabriel.

He still wouldn't call her by her not-so-new name of Amira.

"I haven't seen you much lately," said Gabriel. "You have been in Waldmeer a lot."

"Do you miss me?" said Amira.

"No, no, it's not that," said Gabriel.

Amira smiled.

"Now that Charlie has sold her property, I have been thinking how much I miss my trips to the back hills of Waldmeer," said Gabriel. "It was so good for me as an artist. The peace and quiet inspired me in a different way from what I get in the city. It was special."

"Yes, it was a special time," said Amira, thinking of it fondly.

Both were silent for a moment, and then Amira suddenly said, "I have an idea. Why don't you rent my bungalow? You can set it up as a studio. You can have cheap rent because when I moved to the share house in Eraldus, you helped me for a whole year."

"Done deal," said Gabriel without hesitation.

In the space of a few moments, a new happy plan was set in place.

AT THE NEXT Bungalow Buddies meeting, the convenor asked each resident how they got on with finding a tenant.

Ide spoke when it was her turn, "I have someone, thank you."

That was all she said. She wasn't a big talker. Amira briefly saw the translucent man standing behind Ide with his hand on her shoulder. As Amira had by now suspected, it was Fabian. She could not tell Ide that he had been around lately, but one day, she would. That was the last time Amira saw Fabian.

"That's wonderful news," said the convenor. "Everyone in the Bungalow Buddies has managed to find a renter."

A sense of accomplishment fell over the group. By working together with a gracious spirit, they had quite easily created something that would benefit everyone.

"Until next time, my friends," said the convenor.

A ray of goodness spread out from the little group into the town. Amira walked up to Ide and put her arm through hers on the way out of the meeting.

"Buddy," said Amira, smiling.

"We *are* buddies," said Ide, "bungalows or not."

She held onto Amira's arm more tightly than she needed to.

"So, who is your tenant?" said Amira.

"The guy from Charlie's property," said Ide.

"Really?" said Amira.

"Yes, I was a bit surprised," said Ide. "He called at my house and said he had heard I had available accommodation. I showed it to him and told him the price. He said it was too much for an old bungalow. When I replied that he could have it for half price if he fixed it up a bit, he said he would take it."

"That's great," said Amira.

"He did add that he wouldn't be there for long," said Ide.

"It doesn't matter. It's all good," said Amira. "Anyway, time will tell."

"I hope we don't bother him," said Ide, a little worried. "He said that he is used to keeping to himself. I don't want my son to start annoying him."

"Oh, don't worry about that," said Amira. "I'm sure you will both do him a world of good."

Ide is more polite than I, thought Amira. *Farkas will find it easier to cope with her.*

There was something else Amira wanted to find out.

"Do you feel okay about him being there?" said Amira. "I mean, not everyone in the town likes him. Do you?"

Amira looked directly at Ide and waited for the answer. She knew that instinct was the great director in the formation of all relationships.

"For some reason," said Ide, "I do. I don't know why. I just do."

"Then," said Amira, "it's a done deal."

REACH FOR IT

CHAPTER 11
DONE OR DIFFERENT

Amira carried the last art supplies from Gabriel's car down the winding track to the bungalow. He had been driving to Waldmeer the previous few weekends as he was keen to fix up the bungalow as a country studio.

"Thanks a lot, Maria," said Gabriel. "Anywhere on the floor is fine."

"Okay," said Amira. "I'll leave you to it. I'm sure you have lots to do."

She turned for the door, which was only two steps away. The entire length of the bungalow was no more than ten steps, probably eight of Gabriel's. It was just enough room for a bed and a small kitchen table. One single cupboard and sink made up the kitchen. Next door was a tiny room with an old but adequate bathroom. Running along one entire wall was Gabriel's art and sculpting equipment.

As the floor was uneven, he had bits of wood underneath everything. The wood was constantly reshuffled to stabilise the structures.

Amira looked back as she closed the bungalow door, expecting Gabriel to be staring at his works of art, all at various stages of completion. She was surprised to see that he was, instead, staring at her.

She stopped walking and asked, "How's it all going? Are you happy with what you are making?"

"Truth be told, I'm not. I don't know what's wrong exactly, but I'm not happy with any of it," said Gabriel.

Amira stepped back into the room and touched some of the clay. It was harder than she expected. He must not have been working with it for some time.

"I feel that most of my best work was done a few years ago at Charlie's property," continued Gabriel. "Maybe, I'm done."

He sat on the bed in exasperation, throwing his arms in the air and falling back.

"Maybe all the art in me is used up. I'd better think of another job fairly soon, or I might have to live in this little bungalow permanently."

Amira laughed and said, "Don't worry. I'm sure you won't have to live here like the local fringe dweller."

She walked over to the window. The wood around the frame was worn and rough, but serviceable. In the distance, she could see the ocean between the trees. It looked still and calm from up here.

"Perhaps, you are not 'done' but different," she said. "You are not the same man you were a few years ago. Maybe you need to find out who you are now."

"That could take a long time," said Gabriel.

"What is the problem, exactly?" asked Amira. "Is it that you can't think of what you want to create, or don't like anything you make?"

Gabriel pulled himself up off the bed.

"If I start working on a piece the way I used to, before long, I feel as if it's..." he paused as he searched for the right word. "You know I'm not good with words."

He slumped back on the bed.

"Your words are fine. Reach for what it is you want to say," said Amira.

After a moment, Gabriel said, "Empty," with the irritation of someone who had discovered an unwelcome visitor living in his house.

"Empty?" said Amira.

"Not enough," said Gabriel, still annoyed at his discovery. "What once seemed enough doesn't seem enough anymore."

"That's because you've changed," said Amira. "What satisfied you before doesn't satisfy you now. You have more in you, and you won't feel right unless you find it—and express it."

"How do I do that?" asked Gabriel. "I've tried, but I seem to get nowhere."

"Be braver. Be more honest," said Amira. "Don't hold onto what you used to know. You're an artist—you're meant to express what other people can't. What's true for you now will take more courage."

CHAPTER 12
WHO ARE YOU?

The next day, Amira was packing to return to Eraldus. Gabriel walked up the hill from the shops and sat on the grass beside her car.

"Are you also leaving this afternoon?' asked Amira.

"No, I'm going to stay a few more days. I need some more time alone."

"I wish I could stay here in Waldmeer, too," said Amira. "These days, I feel so at peace here that I have to make a big effort to go back to the city."

"You are peaceful whether you are here or in Eraldus," said Gabriel, not entirely pleased with this observation. "Do you even need anyone else in your life?"

"Is that why you won't call me Amira? Because you think Amira doesn't need anyone and Maria does?"

"Sometimes, Maria was strange," said Gabriel unapologetically, "but I felt that she was, sort of, manageable. Now, I'm not sure I even know who you are."

He looked down at the grass and wondered if he would regret those words.

Amira did not want to dismiss his words lightly. They had a lot of truth in them. She was very different from the girl he first met years ago, and even very different from the prehospital-Homeland transition eight months ago. She wondered what she could say to acknowledge his feelings, but let him know it was nothing to be concerned about. There was much she would love to tell him, but she could not. He would not understand it. And far from reassuring him, it would scare him. Suddenly, the seriousness left her. She smiled, walked over to Gabriel, and took his hand.

"We are both here, aren't we?" said Amira.

Gabriel didn't know what she meant or how that was supposed to make him feel better. Amira hugged him and got in the car. He didn't hug her back because he already felt too vulnerable.

CHAPTER 13
IT'S GOOD

I t was Wednesday night.

Three days on, thought Gabriel, *and I haven't thought of a single creative idea.*

He turned the light off and lay in bed. He didn't bother closing the curtain as no one could see in. However, he could see out.

His eyes accustomed themselves to the dark. The mass of luminous stars started to make their presence known. The longer he looked, the more radiant they became.

Before closing his eyes, he sent a request to those majestic stars: *You light-bringers that give so much, why don't you tell me what I should bring?*

~

In another dimension:

What is this place? Gabriel wondered as he found himself amongst grand trees, luscious grass, dazzling water, and sublime colours.

There was an overriding feeling of beauty, synchronicity, and happiness everywhere around him.

He was vaguely aware that it was a dream, but it was so vivid and meaningful that he didn't care what it was.

For several hours, he was completely immersed in a sense of wonder and deep satisfaction.

⁓

THE LAST STAR bid its farewell as Gabriel looked through the bungalow window. It was morning, and he was awake.

Wow, that was astonishing, he thought. *I hope I don't lose the memory of it.*

Instinct told him to stay close to nature to hold onto it for longer. He walked down to the town, and everything looked brighter. He passed several young boys, laughing and chasing each other with their skateboards. They seemed so full of joy. The shopkeepers and customers all seemed happier than ever he had seen them. The morning could not have been more perfect.

Turning his mind to work, he noticed that the effects of the previous night were already starting to fade. He knew it was a temporary offering from the stars, yet the dream still had such a palpable residue in him that he wondered if he had somehow misunderstood life in all his previous years.

Perhaps we are mistaken, he thought, *to think our life is so concrete and material. I have never felt anything to have more reality, vibrancy, and importance than I did last night.*

Instead of turning to his sculptures, Gabriel went to the cupboard and pulled out a canvas and oils. He had not painted for many years. The painting seemed to paint itself.

In one day, he had substantially completed the most impressive artwork he had ever done.

Even if no one else likes it, I know it's good, he thought.

By Friday morning, Gabriel's normal consciousness had, for the most part, returned. It was inevitable, and he didn't begrudge it. As he was packing up to leave in the afternoon, a neighbour walked to the front gate.

"You must be Gabriel," said the woman. "Amira told me that you are in the bungalow. Is she back from the city yet? I want to let her know about the upcoming church fete."

"Not yet," said Gabriel. "She will probably be a few more hours. I will let her know that you called."

Gabriel folded the note letting Amira know about the neighbour and started to write *Maria* on the outside. He remembered the dream, crossed out *Maria*, wrote *Amira* instead, slid it under her door, and headed back to the city.

THE CONVENT AND
THE CLINKERS

CHAPTER 14
THE CONVENT

Amira's neighbour had recently let her know about the forthcoming church fete and festivities to commemorate the one-hundredth anniversary of the Convent. It was a place Amira loved. Inscribed on the heavy wooden door of the Convent were the words:

Built on the hill to be close to God.

It wasn't difficult to find a hill in Waldmeer.

Originally, the order was enclosed. They did not interact with the outside world. Their life was prayer. Amira felt the very air inside still carried the sacred energy of their prayers. She didn't go there too often. She had to remain in the world.

In the early days, the nuns grew much of their own food in a large garden. The priest would take the excess each Friday and sell it at the weekend market, along with the sisters' candles.

Whenever Amira visited the Convent, she passed a row

of paintings of the founding sisters. The one in the middle was Sister Geraldine. Something about the pictures fascinated Amira. She often said hello to them by name as she passed. Even she didn't expect them to answer. But one day, Sister Geraldine did.

She told Amira that she had come from Ireland.

"I told God that if I could be of service to anyone in the world, my soul would be happy," said Sister Geraldine. "He brought me here to Waldmeer."

Although the order was enclosed, Sister Geraldine said that, eventually, it was time to educate the children of the logging families.

The day came when the sisters would step out into public life.

The nuns always sat behind a curtain in the church, unseen by the congregation. One Sunday morning, the sisters walked into the curtained area and sat down as usual. Then Sister Geraldine stood up and, with a touch of drama, opened the curtains. She had a sense of humour.

The congregation collectively gasped as they witnessed the unveiling of the holy sisters.

The sisters got the giggles.

And so began their public life of service.

And serve, they certainly did.

CHAPTER 15
THE CLINKERS

Although the sisters were now educating the children of Waldmeer and the surrounding areas, they were forbidden to teach the Clinker children who lived in the back hills. Their camps shifted with their parents' movements. The instruction came from the Bishop, and the sisters were bound to obey.

The Clinkers had appeared in Waldmeer around the time of the forest loggers. They were a cross between gypsies and monks. Although they were a deeply spiritual people, it manifested in ways foreign to Waldmeerians—dancing, chanting, magic, healing, living in nature, and free-spiritedness.

The women usually wore red veils in town, with lots of jewellery and small, clinking bells. That was how they came to be called the Clinkers. No one thought to ask their real name. The townsfolk preferred the nickname. It carried the suggestion of belonging in jail.

Many were suspicious of their magic and healing, and

some of the Clinker boys would steal from the townsfolk. The boys were quick and stealthy—no match for townspeople. The elders tried to keep them in line, but every group has its trouble spots.

Sister Geraldine was fond of the Clinkers and possibly a little envious of their freedom. She would have loved to run barefoot through the forest, sing with the trees, and befriend the creatures.

At one point, six Clinker children were brought to the Convent by their mother. She refused to speak to anyone except Sister Geraldine. The children were fatherless, and the mother was ill. She said she was going to the city for treatment. She did not want the children to be raised by the other Clinkers. She wanted them educated, not raised only in the ways of the forest.

Sister Geraldine explained that she was not allowed to take the children.

The woman, who read minds more than she minded words, looked at Geraldine with the determined eyes of a forest creature protecting her young and said, "You are their mother now."

She then left.

Sister Geraldine told the other sisters that the children were orphaned from a Waldmeer farming family. Everyone knew it wasn't true, but Geraldine wanted to spare the sisters from breaking their vow to the Bishop. She felt bound to a higher order.

The other sisters were thrilled to have children living with them. After all, they would have been mothers if not for their religious decision. They immediately got to work and enclosed the long verandah, scraping together six makeshift beds.

The children slept in those beds for three years.

Then, their mother returned, and the children needed to go back to their family. The youngest child was only a toddler when she first came to the Convent. She did not recognise her Clinker mother and refused to leave Sister Geraldine, whom she considered her rightful mother.

Sister Geraldine kept taking the child to her mother in the back hills, gradually getting her used to her biological family. Each time she returned alone, the other sisters knew not to ask. They all missed the baby.

The little girl spent much of her childhood returning to the Convent. As an adult, she emigrated to Ireland, Sister Geraldine's homeland. There, she married and had children of her own. Eventually, she had ten grandchildren.

The youngest of them was Ide!

Ide had no idea of her connection to the Convent or Sister Geraldine as her adoptive great-grandmother. Certainly, she never dreamed she had Clinker blood in her.

All of this was told to Amira, piece by piece, whenever she passed Sister Geraldine's painting in the Convent hallway.

Amira had to think of a way of telling Ide without saying, *Oh, by the way, I've been talking to your dead, adoptive great-grandmother, and she wants you to know who you are.*

Like Sister Geraldine, Amira decided that a white lie was preferable to a fatal truth, so she told Ide she had found the Convent records and read about Ide's ancestry there.

Thus began Amira and Ide's frequent visits to the Clinkers. They usually visited on ceremony nights and couldn't have had more fun with all the dancing, singing, laughing, magic, and healing. It was very theatrical, but most religions carry a good deal of drama.

The Clinker blood in Ide was thickening with remarkable speed.

CHAPTER 16
LITTLE LIGHT

I de mentioned the Clinkers to Farkas, expecting him to have no interest. To her surprise, Farkas told her he had also been spending time with some of the Clinkers. She had never seen him there and didn't understand why he would be. He was not religious or spiritually minded, nor one to go looking for friends, and the Clinkers were not an obvious choice.

Ide never questioned Farkas. Whatever he chose to tell her was enough. Having Farkas in the bungalow was working well, and Ide did not want to sabotage it. Not least because her son, Christopher, was becoming attached to him.

Christopher would stride down the driveway to the bungalow with legs that seemed to grow an inch every week. Ide sometimes worried that he would be broken-hearted when Farkas decided it was time to go, but she had known enough loss to understand that holding back from life's joys for fear of their ending only means missing them.

Although Ide never questioned Farkas about his association with the Clinkers, she did ask one of her Clinker girlfriends.

"Oh, yeah," said the friend, "he's been hangin' out with *the lost ones*."

"The lost ones?" queried Ide.

"Himach and that lot," said the friend, "those weed guys. The elders call them *the lost ones* because they say that they have taken the freedom of the Clinkers and turned it into trouble with their drug-taking and irresponsible ways. They are the ones giving the Clinkers a bad name. Farkas is an adult. He is free to make his own choices, but if I were you, I'd make sure they don't get their hands on Christopher. Some of our teenage boys have lost their way through them. They waste years of their lives telling themselves the drugs do not affect them, while all along, they are sedating themselves for much of their waking lives. The elders say they are wasting the gift of life and that it is an insult to the Great Life Energy."

Remembering the Clinker code of love, she said, with sadness in her eyes, "I get angry with them, but it is because they are my brothers. I've seen too many of them destroy themselves."

That evening, Ide saw Farkas in the back garden and said quietly, "I don't want Christopher near any of those Clinker weed-boys."

There was a determination in her voice that surprised Farkas. It was the same determined voice of the mother who had once left her children with Sister Geraldine (Ide's biological great-grandmother).

"Relax, it's only marijuana," said Farkas. "It's not like a real drug."

Ide cut him off. "I don't want Christopher in the bungalow when it's there."

Farkas shrugged and walked off as if it was a fuss about nothing, but he knew she was right. At that moment, a little light of love for Ide grew in his heart.

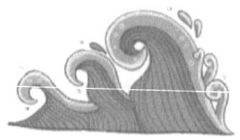

CHAPTER 17
SECONDER

"I'm sorry, Amira, but unless you have a seconder, the matter cannot be put before the assembly," said the Convenor, knowing full well that no one would second it.

Amira was at the meeting for the upcoming one-hundredth anniversary of the Convent. This would be the year's social highlight for Waldmeer, so it was not just church people who were present. Business owners, council members, townsfolk, and those associated with the Convent were all there. Everyone was represented except the Clinkers. One had to have an invitation to attend, and they were not invited.

Amira knew they wanted to be involved and decided it was time to press the town on this divisive issue. However, she couldn't find a suitable seconder for the motion, which meant it could not even be tabled for voting.

"I will second it," said a strong female voice up the back.

Amira couldn't see who it was, but the voice sounded familiar.

The Convenor looked stunned but composed himself and said, "Alright, your name, please?"

"Verloren Reisenden," said the woman. "My husband and I have a holiday house here in Waldmeer. I will second Amira's motion."

No one was more shocked than Amira. As it unfolded, it was due to Verloren that there was a positive outcome for the Clinkers. It was not just that she had made it possible for the motion to be put before the assembly. That was the first step, but it was still unlikely to pass. Verloren was no fool when it came to people politics.

"You may be aware of the successful business my husband and I run in the city," said Verloren. "As is appropriate these days, we always have a policy of inclusion regarding such matters."

Whether the townsfolk knew of her business or not, they could tell that Verloren was a woman of means and business standing. Whatever she said, they were willing to accept in acknowledgement of her superior judgment in the situation.

If Amira alone supported the Clinkers, the people would have dismissed it as the peculiarities of a well-meaning but incomprehensible person with a questionable profession. If she weren't a local, born and bred from good ol' Lenny the fisherman, she would have probably been lumped in with the strange Clinkers.

"Thank you, Verloren," said Amira after the meeting.

Amira knew it was a fragile situation and that Verloren could easily return to her previous hostile position, so it seemed best to say little.

Verloren dismissed Amira, saying, "I don't like nastiness. Besides, the Clinkers are known to me personally."

None of that had much truth in it. Verloren didn't like

nastiness towards herself, but she could be as nasty as the best of them. Nor did she know the Clinkers personally. She may have had a vague knowledge that the Clinkers were somewhere in the hills, but she would neither have understood nor had any alignment with their type of spirituality. However, it didn't matter.

What did matter was that Verloren had decided to use her considerable personal magnetism and force-to-be-reckoned-with nature for a good cause. It was, indeed, a surprise that the good cause was Amira.

"I heard Farkas is living at the bottom of my street," said Verloren tentatively.

"Yes, he is," said Amira. "Close to his old house, where you are now. He's at Ide's."

She wanted to add, *But don't go there. It can only lead nowhere good.*

Instead, she touched Verloren's arm lightly and said, "You look like you are doing really well. So, whatever you are doing, keep doing it."

UNFORESEEN
CIRCUMSTANCES

CHAPTER 18
LAUGHING AT A FUNERAL

"Guess what, Amira," said Gabriel excitedly on the phone.

"I don't know. It sounds good," said Amira, enjoying Gabriel's happiness.

"Come on," urged Gabriel. "You're a healer. You're supposed to be psychic."

"Only sometimes," smiled Amira.

She had no idea what his good news was, but not wanting to spoil his fun, she ventured, "Hmm, my powers are telling me that..."

She paused, waiting for a suitable idea to pop into her mind.

"You sold your painting for a large fortune."

"Nope. Guess again," said Gabriel.

"For a small fortune?"

"No, not even close," said Gabriel, getting annoyed that she wasn't on the same thought track as him.

"What is it then? You will have to resort to telling me," said Amira.

"I got married!" beamed Gabriel.

Amira almost dropped the phone.

Married? she thought incredulously.

"Isn't it wonderful?" purred Gabriel.

"Yes," said Amira weakly. "But to who?"

"What are you talking about? To Paul, of course," said Gabriel.

When Maria/Amira moved to Eraldus a few years ago, she shared a large inner-city house with Gabriel, Charlie, and Mary. When Amira inherited a rundown house from her deceased great-aunt Rose, she moved into it, and Paul took her room in the share house. Paul was one of Gabriel's gay friends. Amira recollected that Gabriel and her worst argument happened when Paul had manipulated Gabriel into saying that Amira meant nothing to him other than as a casual housemate. The memory of it still had some sting.

"I see," said Amira, searching to make sense of what Gabriel was telling her.

How could I have missed this? she thought. *What else have I missed?*

"You sound surprised," said Gabriel.

"I knew you were dating him," said Amira, "but I didn't realise it was so serious."

"Why wouldn't you realise?" said Gabriel. "We have been together since you moved out of the house."

"You rarely talk about him," said Amira. "So, I thought he wasn't that important to you."

"Well, he is. He is my husband," said Gabriel. "You are not being homophobic, are you?"

"That's silly," said Amira. "You know that I don't see people as bodies. You are entitled to everything that everyone else is."

You are entitled, she thought, *to all the same stupid mistakes as everyone else.*

In another world where communication is transparent and honest, Amira would have been able to say, *My concern has nothing to do with sexual orientation. My concern is that I don't think you love him. Not enough, anyway.*

Unable to say that, Amira could think of nothing else to say.

Breaking the uncomfortable silence, Gabriel said, "We love each other, have great fun together, our interests are the same, and seldom fight. We aren't that young anymore. After speaking about it, we agreed that there is no one else for either of us and that we should take the plunge and start making memories together as a team."

"That's great," said Amira, not accustomed to outright lying.

"Don't worry, we'll still have lots of time together," said Gabriel. "Paul wants to come with me whenever I travel to Waldmeer so the three of us can spend time together when we are there. It'll be a bit squishy for two people in that little bungalow. But, hey, we are newlyweds. It'll be cosy."

Amira laughed. It felt like laughing at a funeral.

"I look forward to it," she said.

The last thing she wanted to do was spend time with Gabriel and Paul together. She had to search for qualities in Paul that she liked, and did not like the person Gabriel became around him. She pulled herself together, feeling that any moments spent with Gabriel were precious and fast declining.

"Thank you for telling me," said Amira. "I appreciate it. I'll let you go now. I'm sure you have lots to do."

It was a defining moment for Amira, one of those

surprises life can throw our way that leave us searching for meaning. She got off the phone and walked to her favourite chair. It was the one where she read and prayed, where the angels gathered. She sat down and cried.

CHAPTER 19
TURNAROUND

Although with Verloren's unexpected intervention, Amira had a victory with the church council about the Clinkers, it was short-lived. Less than two weeks later, she received a letter from the town council telling her she could no longer practice as a healer in Waldmeer.

> The town protocol clearly states that no one is to conduct a business that is seen to undermine the reputation of Waldmeer as a leading tourist destination. As numerous residents have complained about the appearance of an unprofessional business of dubious nature, we regret to inform you that you cannot conduct your business as a healer in the vicinity of Waldmeer. We trust that you will cooperate with our instructions immediately. As our decision is final, we will not enter into any further correspondence.

Cowards, thought Amira. *Do I not have the right of reply? And what complaints? From whom? Is the council calling me a charlatan?*

She knew that they were repaying her for helping the Clinkers. Courage always has a price. It doesn't come for free. It was a large price, but Amira felt it was not for her to say what it would be. With a heavy heart, she took down her sign from the front gate and told herself that she would have to be satisfied with her practice in Eraldus.

Amira told Ide about the letter from the Council. Ide, in turn, told Farkas. Farkas, in turn, told the Clinker guys he had been seeing lately. For all their faults, *the lost ones* were not lost in every way. They were men with the fire of *this will not do* inside them. Generally, however, it tended to get focused in the wrong direction. Not this time. The Clinker guys decided, with Farkas, to approach the Chairman of the Council. They knew where he lived. It was dark and quiet as they stood at his door one evening. The Chairman was far from at ease when he opened the door to the wild-looking Clinker men. He went to shut the door, but Farkas came from the back of the group and put his foot in the doorway.

"They have something to tell you," said Farkas.

The Chairman recognised Farkas from town and visibly relaxed.

He looked at Himach, the Clinker spokesman, and said, "What is it then? What do you want from me?"

"We know the trouble with Amira is not about her," said Himach, "but us. If you let her have her practice and don't stop our mothers and sisters from being involved with what they want in the town, then we will move on."

"Will you?" said the Chairman, thinking this would make many townsfolk happy.

"Not all of us," said Himach. "Just us young guys. We are the ones you don't like. Leave our families to live in peace, and we will go to the Flatlanders."

"The Flatlanders?" said the Chairman.

"Yep," said Farkas. "That's what they call the city dwellers."

Himach and the young men were itching for a change, and the idea of the Flatlanders seemed much more fun than the boring back hills of Waldmeer.

"We do not compromise our high standards under threat or bribery," said the Chairman, pulling himself tall.

He knew that this group of Clinkers were the drug takers and, sometimes, dealers. Getting rid of them would be a great advantage to the town.

"But I suppose the Council would be willing to reconsider its decision under unforeseen circumstances," he added.

Farkas turned to Himach and said, "It's enough. Let's go."

AFTER A FEW DAYS, Amira got another letter from the Council saying they had reconsidered their decision because the complaining parties had withdrawn their objection. She was now free to practice as a healer. Amira didn't know why, but was grateful for the unexpected turnaround. In the afternoon, she walked to Ide's house and showed her the new letter. Ide was also surprised and equally glad.

"I can't believe that stupid Council came to their senses," said Ide to Farkas that evening. "Wonders never cease."

"People who make mistakes are not all bad," said Farkas mysteriously. "Everyone is learning something."

He turned towards his bungalow, leaving Ide to stare after him.

BEGINNINGS
AND ENDINGS

CHAPTER 20
BOOKSHOP

Amira was a frequent visitor to the quaint Waldmeer bookshop. She would scan the shelves to see what people were writing and reading, then sit on the old upholstered chair in the corner with anything that interested her. As she rarely bought any books, she tried to think of another way to repay the owner, Teresa, who had recently taken over the shop.

Teresa was originally a local of Waldmeer, but she had been living in the city for many years. She left Waldmeer when she married a wealthy businessman. Amira thought that money and Teresa were not an obvious match. Although she had a wardrobe full of *rich clothes,* she preferred to wear the ones she got from the op shop. At forty, she still wore her long brown hair in plaits tied with strips of leather. The vintage clothes and the long braids made her look like a bohemian, which she probably was. Her family were farmers, and they were in no way remarkable. Everyone was surprised when she initially attracted Arthur's attention, her future husband. Twenty years older than

Teresa, he was sophisticated and worldly-wise. If it had not been for Arthur's mid-life crisis and a conscientious effort at finding a meaningful path, neither would have ever come into contact with the other.

After professional success and marital failures, Arthur decided that a move to the country would help him find a new direction in life. He bought a house in Waldmeer and ran his business from there, with frequent visits to the city and abroad. A sharp intellect meant that Arthur read every trailblazing book that might help him with his mission. He was a regular customer of the bookshop and their biggest buyer. The bookshop was where Arthur and Teresa first met. Initially, Teresa was intimidated by him. However, she was also intrigued. She was certainly flattered by his interest. Arthur soon realised that Teresa had a good heart and a bright mind. She was young and, unlike Arthur, had little baggage from life. He decided that together, they could start from scratch and create the family life he longed for. Thus, the beginning of their fifteen-year journey.

CHAPTER 21
MORE OR LESS

"Do you remember the old bookshop?" said Teresa one morning as Amira browsed the biographies.

"Yes, sure," said Amira. "This bookshop has been here as long as I can remember."

Amira pointed in a complimentary fashion to Teresa's new decor and said, "It didn't look like this."

"From about twelve, I would come here on my way home from school," said Teresa. "My parents didn't have money, but even if they did, I don't think they would have seen the value of spending it on books. In all the years I came here as a schoolgirl, I only ever bought one book, and that was because of Mr MacArthur. When he was the new principal at school, he gave me an award. It was a book voucher. I think the bookshop manager told him about my many visits, and Mr MacArthur probably invented the award so he could give it to me. I used to tell myself that, one day, I would have enough money to buy hundreds of books."

"Little did you realise," said Amira, "that it wasn't that far in your future and you would have not only enough money for any book you wanted but also anything else you wanted."

"I wasn't overly interested in Arthur's money," said Teresa. "I felt that too much money was alienating."

She watched an elderly couple waiting at the bus stop. She enjoyed ordinary people.

"Our relationship wasn't a passionate love affair," continued Teresa. "It was more of a love affair with his books."

She hugged some of the books on her counter in mock dramatic fashion.

"The first time I visited Arthur's house and walked into his hallway, I was in awe. Rows and rows of beautiful books lined every wall. They represented a new world to me, and I was willing to work with whatever that meant in terms of the relationship."

Two customers walked in, and Teresa turned to serve them.

"Before I left Waldmeer," said Teresa when the shop was empty again, "my aunt said to me, 'It is generally not first-generation rich people who have *the problem*. They can usually remember where they came from. It's the second generation.' She didn't say what *the problem* was exactly, but spoilt, delusional, and obnoxious sprang to mind."

Amira smiled. "Yes, they can be the problems of poor little rich kids, but your kids have none of that."

"The money brought me experiences that otherwise would have been totally inaccessible," said Teresa. "And it educated me about many things. Having had it, I now know it is unnecessary to feel less than anyone with money or power. And God help me if I ever think anyone is less than me." She paused. "In the beginning, Arthur was very sincere about his newfound path in life. But it was not maintainable for more than a year or so. It was a rather long, drawn-out, and lonely demise. For sure, the marriage gave its blessings, but it was more of a blessing when it was over."

"You have two beautiful daughters," said Amira warmly. "They are happy here at the school, and you have work that you love. You are still young. You will have another relationship."

"Oh God no," said Teresa emphatically. "I only have enough energy for my kids and my work."

"Perhaps," said Amira, "but men have something to offer that children and work do not."

"I'm not interested in *that*," said Teresa.

"I don't mean 'that' particularly," said Amira as if to entice Teresa back from the land of the renunciate. "Although 'that' is great if things work out that way."

"What then?" asked Teresa.

"Connection. Love," said Amira. "It's a different love to children and work. It will infuriate you, make you cry, make you afraid, and challenge you in every way."

"You are not doing a very good job of selling it," laughed Teresa.

"I don't need to," said Amira. "You already know its worth."

Amira walked towards the door and said, "Next time I come, I'd love to hear what has come your way."

She said it as if it would now be so. Teresa was unsure whether she wanted it, even if it did come her way. Yet, something about the whole conversation seemed to have its own life force.

CHAPTER 22
PRIZE

A few days later, Amira saw Thomas MacArthur in the supermarket.

"Have you been into the bookshop since Teresa has taken it over?" asked Amira.

"No, not yet," said Thomas. "I heard it is looking great. I often see her girls at school, but I haven't caught up with Teresa since her return to Waldmeer. How has she been getting along since her divorce?"

"She's going well," said Amira. "She told me about when you gave her a book voucher as a prize."

"I can't remember that," said Thomas, "because I have probably given ten thousand prizes by now."

He didn't want to count how many years he had been at Waldmeer Secondary School, let alone how many prizes he had given.

"Teresa was a thinker with a lot of potential," said Thomas, "even though there was never much culture in her home. Not to discredit her family, but that's just how it was."

"Why don't you call in and look at the shop?" said Amira.
"I will," said Thomas.

CHAPTER 23
A LITTLE PRAYER

Amira didn't return to the bookshop for a few weeks. When she did, it was crowded with tourists. No one was in the upholstered chair, so she sat with a book. Time must have passed because the shop was empty when she next looked up, and Teresa was looking at her from the counter.

"What's been happening?" asked Amira expectantly.

"Mr MacArthur," said Teresa, "Err, I mean, Thomas has been in quite a few times, and a few days ago, he asked me on a date."

"What did you say?"

"I said 'yes' because you can't say 'no' to the Principal," laughed Teresa. "Seriously, though, after he came in a few times, I realised how much I enjoyed talking to him. He's an attentive listener and kind to my kids at school. I probably need a friend."

As soon as Thomas saw Teresa in the bookshop, he was interested in her. After a few more visits, he was plotting in the harmless way a man like him plots. Normally, Thomas never thought about his ex-students as potential dates or girlfriends. However, in the case of Teresa, he knew that her ex-husband was the same age as him, so he thought it might be a possibility. She was the first woman he had been interested in since Kathleen left.

"That's terrific," said Amira, picking up her shopping bags.

She felt it was an answer to her little prayer for Teresa.

"Something else unexpected also happened," said Teresa.

"What?" asked Amira, putting her bags down again.

"I often go out to see my parents on the farm. As they are now elderly, I need to help a bit," said Teresa. "My dad has employed the young guy from next door's farm. His parents are younger than mine, but they have been there just as long. I remember the guy from when he was a boy. When I left, he was fifteen—awkward, skinny, shy, and, you know, a country boy trying to grow up as best as he could."

"Yes," said Amira, encouraging Teresa to continue.

"He's no shy, skinny, awkward boy anymore!" laughed Teresa.

"Oh, I see," said Amira, laughing as well.

"I have been working with him on the farm jobs whenever I am there and...."

"You like him," said Amira, happy to provide the words.

"Yes," said Teresa. "Do you think that's a bad idea? I mean, he's only thirty. I am hardly one to care about age. I think that's obvious. But do you think I am being silly, setting myself up for something bad to happen?"

"What do you like about him?" asked Amira. "Besides his young, good-looking body."

"I enjoy working with him. He's funny," said Teresa. "We

laugh a lot. I haven't laughed that much for ages. He's just glad to be alive. Mostly, it's that *he* seems to like *me*. That means a lot, doesn't it? If the person wants us in their life."

"It's probably the most important thing," said Amira. "Or, at least, the first thing. What is his name?"

"Bryan with a *y,* not an *i,*" said Teresa. "I remember his mother saying when he was a baby that she wanted him to have a more exotic name than the family name of Brian. So, Bryan, it became. That's about the extent of his exoticness, I think."

After a pause, Amira reassessed the situation and continued, "Well, that's a surprise. You have gone from no one to two interested parties. And you like them both."

"Yes, for different reasons, I do," said Teresa. "I'm not sure what to do about that."

"Be honest to both," said Amira. "And see where that leads."

CHAPTER 24
GROWING UP

The following weekend, Amira made sure to visit the bookshop. It was as interesting as a good movie. Besides, she felt she couldn't abandon what she had helped create.

Our thoughts and prayers have so much power, thought Amira. *If people realised this, they would be much more careful where they let their thoughts drift.*

"As you suggested, I decided that honesty was the best approach," said Teresa. "In essence, Thomas said 'yes,' and Bryan had a fit and stormed off saying, 'I don't share.'"

"I see," said Amira. "So, you are left with one man standing."

"I don't know," said Teresa screwing up her nose. "If Thomas so easily agrees to something he probably doesn't want, what else does he say 'yes' to when he wants to say 'no'?"

"True," said Amira.

"And Bryan is only thirty. Men don't grow up till they are forty," said Teresa.

"I wouldn't go around saying that to your male friends," laughed Amira. "But young men are not very patient and tend to be highly jealous."

"I don't think Bryan is done yet," said Teresa. "At least, I hope not. Otherwise, he would have given up very easily."

Teresa looked bothered, and Amira wanted her to know everything was fine.

"Don't worry," said Amira. "Both relationships, whatever form they may take, now and in the future, are already in motion. They are already bringing up the right issues. Regardless of their outcome, they are working in that good-bad, pleasurable-painful way that important relationships do. Keep your eyes on the straight course of love and trust, and it will help move everything in that direction."

UNFINISHED BUSINESS

CHAPTER 25
CAPTIVATED

Thomas was driving to the city for a meeting with fellow principals. However, he also had another meeting, which was of more importance to him. He had arranged to meet Kathleen at a riverside restaurant near her home. It's not that he wasn't interested in Teresa anymore, but he had called into the bookshop a few days ago with an unexpected request.

"Teresa, I know I have arranged to go out with you next week," said Thomas, "but I was wondering if you would mind postponing it for the time being? I have some unfinished business to attend to in the city."

"Of course, whatever suits you," said Teresa, who was rather surprised.

Until now, everything had been heavily weighted by Thomas's obvious interest in her and her yet-to-be-convinced response.

Well, there you go, thought Teresa when Thomas had gone. *Life is full of surprises.*

As Thomas drove along the country bends, he didn't turn

the radio on. Instead, he reflected on the course of his recent thoughts, which had become increasingly focused on Teresa. After discovering that he had a rival in young Bryan, he often found himself lost in plotting how to win Teresa over. However, one morning as he sat on his balcony watching the rosellas with their early tasks, age and wisdom finally had a moment to speak.

"Haven't you noticed how stressed you are?" said Thomas's inner voice.

"Now that you mention it," said Thomas, "I am getting myself in a state."

"And have you noticed," said the voice, "that your physical health has deteriorated lately?"

"Yes," said Thomas, "my energy levels have been diminishing, and I don't feel that well. I don't want to get ill."

"Do you have any idea what the problem might be?" said the voice.

Thomas was about to say *no* when he decided to ask the question properly and listen for a proper answer. Suddenly, as if someone had opened the curtain, he could see the problem.

"Oh, I see," said Thomas. "I am running away, aren't I? I have given up on trying to heal anything with Kathleen and have made myself busy with a new story, imagining it might be less painful and more rewarding."

"Yes," said the voice, "you told yourself that Teresa is a better story. Since its inception, you have not thought about why your relationship with Kathleen broke down and if those same reasons might affect any future relationship."

If Thomas was honest with himself, which he currently was, all he had been thinking about was how to convince Teresa that he was better for her than Bryan. The underlying premise was that if he could win Teresa, he would be happy. He had become a mental captive, although he was not entirely sure who the captor was. Teresa hadn't forced him to think that way. Regardless, he had lost his peace of mind. In retrospect, it all seemed a little embarrassing. It wasn't that the idea of Teresa was foolish, but how he had so easily let his imaginings grow unchecked.

What was I thinking it was going to give me? After all this time, am I so easily fooled? thought Thomas with uneasy humility.

Perhaps it was shame more than humility. Either would do for now. The voice was gone, having done its job.

CHAPTER 26
COOLING OFF

*I*n *Eraldus:*

Two months had passed since Amira had last seen or spoken to Gabriel. She felt that, as he was a newly-wed, she should leave him alone.

We should respect other people's decisions, thought Amira, *even if they seem bad to us. Perhaps we are wrong. Perhaps we are not wrong, but the decision is necessary for the person's growth.*

While Thomas was driving from Waldmeer to the city to see Kathleen, Amira walked to her local cafe in Eraldus and ran into Gabriel.

"Hi," said Amira.

Gabriel smiled, but it was a little forced. Amira wondered if he didn't want to be friends anymore. She sat in her usual spot in the cafe and put her head in the paper as he went to the counter for takeaway. After a few minutes, he came over and sat down. Both were trying to salvage what had so quickly become a fragile relationship.

That which holds us all together, thought Amira, *is very delicate.*

"How are you?" asked Gabriel.

"I'm fine. And you?" said Amira, sounding a little more formal than she could help.

"Yep, great, thanks," said Gabriel.

Amira looked down. She didn't want to have a meaningless conversation. Gabriel looked at the door and seemed to be making an important decision. He visibly braced himself.

"I'm not going that well," he said as if the words had defeated him. "I'm sorry I haven't been in contact, but I've been busy."

"It's alright," said Amira. "You have work, and now you also have Paul to consider."

Thinking it might be best to ask a few questions, she said, "What have you decided to do about the share house? Only you and Paul are there now. Charlie and Mary have bought their own place and..."

She stopped short of saying, *You and Paul share the same bedroom, so you have two empty bedrooms.*

"Paul and I are still in our own rooms," said Gabriel. "I told him that I like my own space."

"We don't have to be on top of each other all the time," said Amira.

She then realised that her phrase "on top of each other" was conjuring up an image for both of them, but the words had already come out.

"Yeah, we are on top of each other," said Gabriel.

In fact, the bedroom issue was a spiky one for him and Paul and had caused numerous arguments.

"We've been looking at houses to buy and signed a contract last week," said Gabriel.

"Wow," said Amira. "Congratulations."

"Yesterday was the last day of the cooling-off period," said Gabriel. "I told Paul I couldn't go through with the contract, so we withdrew our offer."

After signing the buyer's contract of sale, Gabriel woke up in a cold sweat every morning. Finally, he realised that, for whatever reason, he couldn't go through with it. Amira thought that buying a house and committing to a big mortgage with Paul had had more of an effect on Gabriel than marrying him.

"I can't buy a house with Paul," said Gabriel, grabbing his coffee and standing up to leave, "because... because I can't."

Amira sat there on her own for some time.

It is the ongoing interplay between independence and intimacy, she thought. *Push too far into independence, and we disconnect and hurt each other. Push too far into intimacy, and we get afraid of losing ourselves in it. So, we head the other way. Thus, the cycle perpetuates itself.*

A customer broke her train of thought, "Excuse me, Miss. I notice you aren't reading your paper. Would you mind if I took it?"

"Of course," said Amira, who realised she had been hogging one of the two free cafe papers.

As she passed it to him, he smiled and said, "What a lovely morning. I hope you have a beautiful day."

He was a cheery fellow, full of joie de vivre.

"And you too," said Amira.

CHAPTER 27
GAROURINN

I n *Waldmeer:*
Amira rarely spoke about her personal life. Whenever people asked about her life, she said something carefully appropriate. However, Ide was a good soul, self-assured enough not to be jealous of other people's happiness or happy at other people's misery. When Amira next saw her, she confided in her about Gabriel.

"You know how Gabriel got married and hasn't been to Waldmeer since?" said Amira.

"Yes?" replied Ide.

"I saw him in Eraldus during the week," said Amira.

"How is he going?" asked Ide.

"I have a feeling that things are not going well with Paul," said Amira.

"Oh, that's a shame," said Ide. "Perhaps, they will work it out. Lots of couples have problems adjusting to each other in the beginning."

"Perhaps," said Amira.

She kissed Ide on the cheek and said, "Goodbye, love. I'll see you later."

That afternoon, Ide knocked on the bungalow door. Normally, she didn't go to the bungalow. She always let Farkas come to her if he wanted anything.

"I saw Amira at the shops," said Ide, "and she told me that Gabriel and Paul aren't doing very well."

"Of course, they aren't," said Farkas abruptly.

"What do you mean, of course?" asked Ide.

She was confused why Farkas would assume to know such a thing.

"How do you know?" she repeated.

Farkas wouldn't reply and looked angry. Ide was startled. Farkas was never angry with her. She never gave him any reason to be.

The next morning, when it was still dark, Farkas made his bed, gathered his things together, ensured the bungalow was neat, and closed the door. He quietly opened Ide's back door, which he knew was always unlocked, and left a note on the kitchen table.

> I am going away for a little while.
> I left money on the bed.
> If I am gone longer than what the money covers, rent out the bungalow to someone else.
> Farkas

He knew Ide would be upset, and Christopher too. However, he had unfinished business to attend to. He hadn't slept much last night. Finally, at 3.00 a.m., he knew what to do. Go to the Leleks, cross Erdo's old walking bridge, head for the North Country, and visit the wolf pack. The last time he had seen them was three winters ago. It was summer now, so that the weather wouldn't be a problem.

Farkas reached the bridge and felt Erdo's eyes on him, but he did not see him. He wondered if he would remember the way, but as with all those who travel to the North Country, it is not the terrain that gets them there but the state of mind.

Over a few days, the rhythmic nature of uninterrupted walking settled his mind, and he found himself at the North Country pass. Somewhere along the pass, the wolves would meet him. That was what happened last time. He was confident of finding them. He got to the end of the pass, and strangely, he had not seen or felt the slightest inkling of them. As he sat under the shade of a large overhanging rock, he recalled that last time he also sat under a similar ledge in the middle of a ferocious storm, and the Head Gardener of Garourinn appeared and saved him.

"You are wise to call me again," said the familiar voice.

Farkas turned towards the Head Gardener. He was not sure that he *had* called him.

"This time, you will not be with the wolf pack," said the Head Gardener. "Go straight ahead to Garourinn."

With that, he left. Having come so far, Farkas decided to keep walking. After about an hour, his old friend, Milyaket, from the Homeland, appeared by his side. Farkas was very fond of Milyaket. However, she was so ethereal that he mostly had no idea how to relate to her.

"Have you had a good journey?" said Milyaket.

Farkas always behaved around her.

"Yes, thank you," he said.

"I will escort you to Garourinn. The Master wishes to see you," said Milyaket.

"The Master?" asked Farkas.

"There is one above the Head Gardener," said Milyaket. "We call him the Master because he is."

CHAPTER 28
MASTER

In the Garden of Garourinn (inter-dimensional):

They soon passed through the gates of Garourinn. Farkas looked at the sweet cottages mixed amongst the green fields, but sensed they were not for him.

"You will be sleeping in the Master's house," said Milyaket.

Over the hill was a large but unpretentious group of buildings. On entering one of the buildings, Milyaket showed Farkas his room on the second floor.

"The Master will see you when it is time," said Milyaket.

Farkas ate with the other residents and was given various tasks in the house, along with everyone else. The other residents were rather monk-like, with simple clothes and gentle demeanours. They were slightly aloof from him as if it was not their place to engage with him too fully, although they were always pleasant.

The days glided by. Farkas wasn't unhappy to be there. It wasn't exciting, but it wasn't boring. Time was marked by meals, domestic tasks, being in the gardens, and exploring the many different buildings. Next door was an extensive library. As there was no other form of entertainment, Farkas occasionally went to the library and picked up random books. The books were not like ordinary books. They were alive with distinct personalities.

He often passed the prayer hall, which the residents attended several times a day. The stillness from the large hall was so powerful that it seemed somewhat disconcerting to Farkas. One evening, he walked past the prayer hall and heard the unfamiliar sound of crying. Peeking through the door, he saw that one of the monks was distressed. The rest of the monks moved to surround him. Some held hands. Others lifted their hands skywards. Others stood motionless. Little bits of light came from each monk and joined above the distressed monk. The light interweaved and formed a radiant ball of orange and white luminescence. It grew much bigger than the sum of the individual lights from all the monks. The monk stopped crying and sat with a transfixed look on his face. Some of the light reached out a stray arm and touched Farkas lightly. It felt incredibly, deliciously inviting.

It feels so precious, thought Farkas, although *precious* was not a word he would normally use.

As HE WAS ABOUT to go to breakfast the next morning, Milyaket knocked on his door. She always wore flowing gowns, so Farkas never saw her body. He had the impression that she was floating across the floor rather than walking. Her soft green and pink aura made her even more beautiful than usual.

"Today will be your last day with us," said Milyaket.

Farkas hadn't thought about leaving for a while.

"The Master is ready to see you," said Milyaket. "I will take you to him."

They went into a part of the building that he had never noticed. Milyaket stopped at a heavy, dark door and bowed to Farkas.

"Until we meet again," she said.

The door had no handle or lock. Farkas was about to ask how to open it, but it opened of its own accord. When he entered the room, he felt all his movements were magnified. He tried to breathe quietly and walk even more quietly, but he felt like an elephant.

"Sit next to me," said a commanding but kind voice in the corner.

As Farkas's eyes adjusted to the light, he saw a man, perhaps forty years old, sitting on a lounge and looking out over the surrounding mountains. Although Farkas felt he should be nervous at meeting the Master, he felt relaxed. Not relaxed like when we let ourselves deteriorate into lethargy, but relaxed like when we feel loved without having to do anything or be anything.

"You have an unanswered question?" said the Master.

"Yes," said Farkas. "When I was with the wolf pack in the North Country, its leader, Galahad, told me that Maria was my sister under a different name."

He wondered if the issue needed more explanation and added, "Maria now calls herself Amira."

He then felt embarrassed at telling the Master something he, no doubt, already knew.

"You and Amira have shared a number of lives," said the Master. "Some have been on Earth, and some have been elsewhere. More than once, she was your sister and more than once, she was your partner. Whenever she was your sister, things tended to go well. Whenever she was your partner, it ended badly or sadly."

Farkas did not feel better for the information.

"The problem is not whether you have a sister or love relationship," continued the Master without judgment. "The problem is your concept of love. It must be outgrown or, if you prefer, refined. It is my task to help you with this. However, it is a collaborative venture. I cannot help you if you do not allow it."

The Master softly drew his hand over Farkas's hair as if he were bonding with a young child and led him to the door, which opened automatically.

"Love is to free, not to imprison," said the Master.

Usually, those were words Farkas wouldn't entertain for a passing moment, but now they were embedded in his mind. That's what happens when the Master speaks.

IN WALDMEER:

Ide heard a commotion outside. Christopher was calling out excitedly.

"He's back, Mum," yelled Christopher, who was still young enough to blurt out what he really wanted to say uncensored.

Thank God, thought Ide.

She saw Farkas and Christopher walking down to the bungalow, laughing and joking.

"We have some leftover dinner if you want Christopher to get you some," she said.

"Thanks," said Farkas, pushing Christopher towards his mother. "Go get the plate from your mother. And do the washing up for her, too."

He walked into the bungalow and said to himself, *One step at a time.*

COUPLE

CHAPTER 29
HALF-HALF

In Waldmeer:

Ide had spent the last two days trying to make a workable budget. It still wasn't working. Adding to the problem was her difficulty getting full-time work at Waldmeer Hospital. She was an excellent nurse, and the patients often specifically asked for her. She treated everyone with the same care she would with her own relatives. However, the Matron had been at the hospital almost as long as it had been there, or so it seemed. She held onto the full-time positions for the locals. Ide wasn't born in Waldmeer, so Matron did not have her on the *special* list. Besides, the Matron was more than a little jealous of Ide. Not only did the patients love Ide, but it did not go unnoticed that Ide's patients seemed to heal faster and have fewer complications than most other patients. Ide was, after all, a descendant of the Clinkers, and they have healing in them. Matron didn't know about Ide's connection with the Clinkers, and Ide certainly wasn't telling her. It would have given Matron more ammunition, and she already had enough. There seemed to be only one sensible solution.

"I'm going to have to sell the house," Ide said to Farkas. "The mortgage is impossible for me."

Farkas didn't reply. He could see by the expression on her face that she was both serious and upset. At the end of that week, Farkas brought the topic up again.

"That bungalow is too small for me," he said as if Ide had only just mentioned selling the house. "I've had enough of living in it."

"Yes, I understand. You need a proper place," said Ide with resignation.

"I've found one," said Farkas.

"Really?" said Ide, trying to sound cheery but feeling she was losing him faster than anticipated.

"There is an old guy not far from here who is recently widowed," said Farkas. "He hates living in the house without his wife. He wants a quick sale so that he can move to his son's family."

"You are thinking of buying, not renting?" said Ide.

"I have the money," said Farkas. "I don't want to keep renting. The house is fairly rundown. That and the fact that the guy wants a quick sale means it is a good price."

"That's wonderful," said Ide. "You will love having your own home again."

"I haven't finished," said Farkas with mock sternness. "I have the money, but don't want to put that much money into a house again. Also, it has three bedrooms. Too big for me. I don't want to rent the rooms out. You know I can't tolerate people."

"Yes," agreed Ide, knowing that was all too true and wondering where he was leading.

"So," said Farkas, "I thought you might be interested in jointly buying the house with me, half and half. That way, you would at least own half a house for you and Christopher."

Ide sat there dumbfounded.

"You're not that young anymore," Farkas continued with a half-smile. "You have to consider your financial future."

Ide didn't want to make it seem too big a deal in case it made Farkas feel awkward.

"You and I jointly own it?" she queried to make sure she had not misheard him.

"Yes," said Farkas.

"And if, for some reason, it didn't quite work after a while?" asked Ide.

"Then one of us could buy the other out, or we'd sell it," said Farkas.

This was a considerable risk for both of them. Would Farkas be able to tolerate living with Ide and Christopher in the same house? Would Ide be able to tolerate Farkas? In such close proximity, would their relationship fall apart? Could they trust each other financially? And probably most dangerous, what sort of relationship were they getting into? Friends don't jointly own homes. Lovers do, but they were not lovers. She couldn't ask him for clarification. Even if she did, she didn't think he would have an answer. There were, undoubtedly, many more glaring risks than positives. Ide glanced out the window to break the stream of warnings. She remembered her husband, Fabian, who was now in the Homeland. Did she regret the risks she took with Fabian despite all the problems? No. Ide became still, and a cloak of calm seemed to float onto her shoulders. Perhaps it was Fabian.

She turned back to Farkas and said steadily, "I heard today at work that we are getting a new hospital administrator. He is known for modernising everything and removing the old pecking order. There is a good chance that I will be able to get a full-time, permanent position at the hospital. If I do, it would be a great time to buy half a house."

That was all Farkas wanted and needed. He stood up, looking pleased and relieved.

"I'll ring the agent to see when we can look at it," he said.

The following week, they signed the contract. As they walked out of the real estate office, Farkas reached over and kissed Ide on the cheek. He had never touched her, let alone kissed her.

Ide said too quietly for him to hear, but perhaps he did, "God help us both."

CHAPTER 30
SOFT BELLY

Teresa ran her hand slowly down Bryan's back. It was brown and strong. When she reached the small of his back and onto his backside, it changed to white but was just as defined. She smiled at the whiteness of the skin not exposed to long days outside on the farm. He was still waking up.

"Now that Thomas has dumped you, I suppose you have no choice but me," joked Bryan.

"He didn't exactly dump me," protested Teresa.

"I'd say he did," said Bryan. "You were seeing him. He stopped seeing you. In my books, that's dumping."

"Oh, okay," smiled Teresa.

She had heard that Thomas had reconnected with his ex-girlfriend, Kathleen. She was glad for him and hoped it worked out. Bryan reached for Teresa and then poked her soft belly.

"Hey, I have had two children," said Teresa defensively.

She thought she heard Bryan saying that he liked it soft,

but she wasn't sure because his words were muffled by his kissing her belly.

Not surprisingly, Teresa and her ex-husband, Arthur, never had much of a sexual relationship. They were not drawn together that way, and it did not bloom as the years passed. The little sexual contact they had in the earlier years shrivelled into virtually nothing. Until Bryan, Teresa had not experienced a vibrant and close sexual relationship. It was a considerable part of what attracted them, how they bonded, and the enjoyment they derived from each other. They were falling in love with each other's bodies as much as with each other.

Teresa's girls were in the city for the weekend with their father. They didn't know about Bryan. Teresa felt that, at this stage, they didn't need to know. Besides, if they knew, Arthur would also know, and he had a vindictive side. Bryan was no match for someone like Arthur. Arthur was unlikely to find happiness in another relationship due to his unwillingness to learn, so he would likely be vengeful. Teresa knew her enemy and was well prepared to protect her new life and her new love.

However, she had another enemy she was not so well-equipped to fight—Bryan's mother, Clarice. Bryan was the apple of his mother's eye, and she had plans for him. Being involved with an older woman was not one of them. Clarice could hardly manipulate a forty-year-old woman with Teresa's life experience. Teresa made sure to point out to Bryan that Clarice was not her mother and that he must cope with her himself. What made matters worse was that he still lived at home out of the convenience of working on the family farm. It did cross Teresa's mind that Bryan may be too young for her and not mature enough to deal with his mother, but then she would look into his open, transparent, blue eyes and remember that this was his journey as much as hers. They may be learning different things, but they were learning them together. It was enough to know that.

CHAPTER 31
NEED OR LOVE

In the city:

"This is delicious," said Gabriel.

"I knew you'd like it," said Paul. "You always do."

As Gabriel was about to take his dinner plate to the sink, Paul stopped him.

"Sit down for a while," said Paul.

"I've got heaps of work to do tonight. Can we talk later?" asked Gabriel.

"It's important," said Paul.

Gabriel sat down again. The thought crossed his mind that he hadn't looked closely at Paul for a while. Paul looked sad.

"What's the matter?" asked Gabriel.

"This is hard for me to say," said Paul with a quiver. "You see, I love you."

"Of course you do," said Gabriel. "And I love you."

"That's the thing, right there," said Paul. "Do you?"

Gabriel went to speak, but Paul put his hand up.

"I don't want to fight about this," said Paul. "It's too

important. Ever since we met, I have loved you. You are, for me, the perfect mate—handsome, creative, kind, and funny. I couldn't have been more thrilled when you took an interest in me. At the bottom of my heart, I always knew that you didn't quite feel the same way about me as I do about you, but I was willing to take whatever you wanted to give me. Besides, I have lived in the hope of getting you to love me more. I don't think you realise how much it hurts when you pull away from me. It's not just about not buying the house. You do it in a thousand different ways. I tell myself that you are entitled to your independence. If I want to be with you, I have to accept that you need a lot of it. Sometimes, I feel embarrassed when other people think you don't love me. It's humiliating."

Paul stood up, went and got tissues, and wiped his eyes.

"I suppose," said Paul, "to be fair, maybe it is need more than love. I say how much I love you. Perhaps, a great deal of it is need. I feel so much better with you in my life, and I am terrified of losing you. Today, I told myself that trying to get you to love me will never make you love me. That breaks my heart."

Paul nodded to indicate that he was done.

"I don't want to say anything lightly," said Gabriel, "because what you have said deserves a proper response. Let me think about it."

He hugged Paul, and both could not help but feel the other's soul intertwine. Paul felt exhausted and went to bed.

Gabriel watched him and thought, *So much of what he said is probably true. I do push him away, but I can't stand neediness. I would rather be single than feel trapped. But maybe it's more than that.*

Paul rolled over and went into a deep sleep.

CHAPTER 32
LITTLE BOOK OF HEALING

Thomas hadn't seen Kathleen all year. He walked up the steps of the riverside restaurant, telling himself to be calm and breathe. He need not have worried. There was no denying their relationship ended with a rift, but Kathleen was not the sort of woman to hold onto such things. Besides, there was still a lot of love between them. They sat outside on the verandah to enjoy the glorious day. There was much to catch up on. They never had a problem talking to each other. Kathleen reached into her bag. Thomas recognised a familiar green cover.

"Are you reading *The Little Book of Healing*?" asked Thomas. "I have been studying the lessons in it all year. I got it from Amira."

"What a coincidence," said Kathleen. "So have I. My brother, Aishi, gave it to me at the beginning of the year. He has lots of fantastic books at the retreat centre. It has been travelling everywhere with me in my handbag."

"Me too," said Thomas. "Not in my handbag."

His laughter helped him to relax. The thought of them

independently choosing to study the same book gave him courage.

Perhaps, he thought, *we are not as disconnected as I believed.*

"Kathleen," he said, "we need to talk about what happened. I'm not asking you to come back to me, but we are too old to let a good relationship die without giving it every chance to survive. I don't care in what way it survives." He shuffled and lowered his eyes. "Survive, that's all. Not die completely."

Thomas's directness gave Kathleen a little hope that it was worth the emotional effort to talk about it.

"Let's not have a blame talk," she said. "That would only make things worse. However, I do believe that we must be honest with each other. The pain caused in the situation warrants an honest attempt to address it, don't you think?"

"Yes, I do," said Thomas.

"I also don't want to talk about the details of what happened," said Kathleen, "or I am afraid we will get nowhere."

"Agreed," said Thomas.

"For me, the bottom line is that I feel I can't trust you," said Kathleen. "That may come as a surprise because you probably see yourself as a very trustworthy person. In many ways, you are. But in others, you are not."

"I think that is harsh," said Thomas.

"Perhaps," said Kathleen, "but you are asking for my trust, and I don't give it lightly. I must know that the person I am trusting is trustworthy. Otherwise, you will betray me in a thousand small ways, if not big ones."

"I won't try to defend myself," said Thomas. "I can't see myself being that way. However, I trust you are saying this in good will to help us both."

"Yes, that is all I am asking," said Kathleen. "To look at it. To try. If I feel you are trying, then I will be satisfied."

Kathleen said that she would like to go home.

As they hugged goodbye, she asked, "By the way, what lesson are you up to in the book?"

Thomas replied, "The one that says, *We can learn to use the pain in our relationships to transform us, turning them into entities that heal, not harm.*"

"That was my lesson last week," said Kathleen. "We are not too far apart."

PETALS AND SWEET PEAS

CHAPTER 33
ENOUGH

In Waldmeer:

Amira and Ide were sitting at Ide's kitchen table in her new house.

"Sorry, it's still such a mess," said Ide.

"Not at all," said Amira. "It's coming along really well. I must tell you that you have inspired me with a big change. After you explained your budget and how the new house came about, I started to think about my situation. I am very grateful to have inherited not one but two lovely little homes. I doubt I would ever have been able to buy a home myself. However, I thought about how much travel I do back and forth to Eraldus each week. Also, how expensive it is to run two homes and the maintenance. If I only had one home, I could use the money from the other to help as an income. I don't make much money from either of my practices. I always seem to end up doing much of it for free. But I have been given so much, why would I complain? I asked myself if I were only to have one house, which one would I choose? Waldmeer won, hands down. Besides, the Eraldus house is worth much more than the Waldmeer one. It's the land value. So, I will put it up for sale this week."

"What about your city clients?" asked Ide.

"I'm not sure," said Amira. "They can ring me. I will start writing newsletters for them. I don't know how it will work, but life changes. We often have to go with the flow, not knowing its course. Things can change because there is something better or different for us. If we don't follow our leanings, that which once seemed fine will start to feel unsatisfactory and will dismantle because it is not right for us anymore. It becomes a burden rather than the blessing it once was. We must trust that, as we were cared for in the past, we will be cared for in the future."

"It will make your life simpler," said Ide.

"My Great-Aunt Rose would say, 'Enough is ample sufficiency.' One house is enough. And Waldmeer is enough," said Amira.

After a moment, she added, "It's very quiet. Christopher is at school, but where is Farkas?"

"Who knows?" said Ide. "I never ask. I want this to work."

She pointed to the house. But, perhaps, she was pointing to something more than the house. Amira nodded sympathetically.

"I told him you were coming this morning," said Ide.

"What did he say?" asked Amira.

"Nothing," said Ide. "When he left earlier, I asked if he wanted to stay and see you. He said, 'No, you have no idea how annoying she can be. And offensive.'"

Amira laughed.

"You're not offended, are you?" said Ide. "Otherwise, I wouldn't have told you."

"No, of course not," said Amira. "It's true. But I do pick

my people. Or, at least, someone picks them. I'm only annoying (and possibly offensive) if I think the person can cope. Besides, we have a responsibility to give our best to others. Sometimes, our best is not what people want to hear."

"Yes, but if I did that," said Ide, "we'd be ripping up the house contract within a few weeks."

"Absolutely. You just be yourself," said Amira. "That is what is right, and that is what will work."

CHAPTER 34
SACRED AND WORTHY

As Amira reached her gate, she could see Gabriel's car. She reminded herself that as he was renting the bungalow, it was his to come and go as he pleased, with whomever he pleased. She opened the gate and walked along the curving path to her front door.

Waldmeer had ideal weather for gardens. Plenty of sunshine and rain. That was why the rainforest backing onto Waldmeer was so alive and wondrous. Often, Amira would throw seeds around the garden beds, and then, without another thought, they would grow into beautiful flowers within a month or two. It was the easiest gardening ever. She reached down to pick some of the sweet peas bordering the path. They were climbing everywhere, up the roses and over the lavender.

I'll get some of each colour—pink, mauve, red, and white, she thought.

"You don't have any yellow ones," said a voice.

Amira looked up. It was Gabriel. He picked some yellow ones and passed them to her.

"Thank you," said Amira.

"Where have you been this morning?" asked Gabriel.

"I was visiting Ide and Farkas's new house," said Amira.

"Do they have a house together?" asked Gabriel.

"Yes," said Amira.

Gabriel looked confused but shrugged and said, "What's it like?"

"It needs a lot of fixing up, but it will be lovely when done."

Amira stood up and brushed the garden dirt off her clothes.

"Farkas told Ide that I'm annoying and offensive," she said.

Gabriel turned for his car and said over his shoulder, "For once, I'd agree with him."

Later that day, Amira crossed paths with Gabriel again.

No sight of Paul yet, thought Amira. *Perhaps he didn't come.*

"Are you on your own, Gabriel?" she ventured.

"Yes," said Gabriel.

"I have made an important decision," said Amira.

"What is it?" asked Gabriel, wondering if it might also affect him.

"I am going to sell my Eraldus home and live here permanently," said Amira.

Gabriel looked at Amira for a few moments. He remembered that he had found their share house when Amira first moved to Eraldus.

My God, that seems like an eternity ago, he thought.

He wasn't sure what Amira's decision meant for him or if it meant anything at all. He told himself that it was her business.

"Whatever you want," he said and continued walking to the bungalow.

Amira returned to her garden. It was a large cottage garden that had been faithfully cared for by her parents since they built the small fibro house decades ago. She no longer tended the vegetable patch. The hen run at the bottom of the garden was now uninhabited by feathered friends who had all died of old age. The orchard thrived with virtually no care. It was well established and reaped the benefit of her father's nurturing for many years. Amira loved the flower beds. She had a knack with flowers. They grew enthusiastically and spread beauty with minimal attention. That is the whole idea of a cottage garden—unlabored, unpretentious, homely, and reassuring.

Walking through the flowers, Amira reflected, *I do not want to annoy or offend anyone. However, to the ego, it can often be seen that way. It is constantly on guard and looking for all the ways it will be betrayed and hurt. If we listen with our fears, then almost everything is a threat. If we listen with our spirit, then no offence is taken. The voice we listen with changes our perception.*

As she had so much travelling to do, the Waldmeer garden had not infrequently been on the brink of chaos, at which point she would spend a few hours fixing it up so it would be manageable again. It had so many plants, bulbs, and seeds that it could run away with itself very quickly. Now that Amira was about to enter a different phase of her life, when she could settle into the routine of one house and one town, she looked at the garden with fresh eyes. She didn't want to tame it. That would be a shame to tame such a thing. Besides, no matter how wild it got, there was always an invisible, underlying, loose order.

Gardens remind us to be patient and humble because that's

what they are, thought Amira. *They have no delusions of grandeur or plotting schemes. They trust implicitly that they will be cared for as part of the cycle of nature. They give so much, yet they are unaware of their gift. They have no perception of themselves. They treat all their inhabitants, of every type and form, as sacred and worthy. They surrender themselves to the moment with flawless confidence and the unmarred hope of renewal.*

PART II
TOGETHER IN TIME

ONE YEAR ON

CHAPTER 35
ACCIDENT

One year had passed. There had been a little accident. Perhaps, *accident* was not quite the right word, but *little* was. Farkas was standing by Ide's bed in Waldmeer Hospital. They were both staring adoringly at their brand-new baby boy. Farkas had hoped for a little girl, but regardless, the intensity of his feelings of love for and protectiveness over the child surprised him. Ide had secretly known it was a boy. Her Clinker instinct told her. If that had not told her, the look on the ultrasound technician's face many months ago had given it away. She had worked in hospitals too long not to be able to read the silent language of its professionals. Still, they had agreed to let it be a revelation at birth, so Ide kept it in her heart.

It wasn't exactly a planned birth. The sex was not planned, and the pregnancy was even more not planned. After a few months of sharing the same house, Farkas and Ide occasionally slept together. One would have thought that a woman who already had a child, had been married for a decade, and was working in the nursing profession would have had no miscalculation regarding contraception. However, Ide was by nature unsympathetic to drugs. Her instinct was to keep them out of her system. Of course, she did something else instead. She may have been alternative in her thinking, but she wasn't stupid. She knew everything about natural fertility planning and followed it meticulously. Or, so she thought. Perhaps she did follow it correctly, but this little one was determined to come no matter what she did.

When Ide first discovered she was pregnant, she cried for two days. She was stunned, afraid, and worried about the future. They hardly had a conventional, stable situation at home. Only after the two days, when she had reached a point of peace about it, did she tell Farkas. She didn't want to have to deal with his reaction until she was strong enough. He said nothing for a week. He thought about leaving and told himself he didn't want a child. He wasn't worried about the child's future. He knew that, come rain or shine, Ide would be there for that child. He was worried about his capacity and readiness to be a father. By the week's end, he decided to give it a go. Besides, he told himself that the wheel was already in motion.

"The child is coming whether you stay or leave," said Ide. "My path is already set. I would like you to stay, and the baby would want that too. However, it is your choice. I will not hold it against you if you go."

"I will stay for now," said Farkas. "I'm sorry, but honestly, that's the best I can promise at the moment."

"When you first moved into the bungalow, you said the same," said Ide. "You are still here."

After that, Farkas relaxed and let himself enjoy the whole process. Every time he felt the fear and anxiety come up, he reminded himself that he was not trapped and that everything could even work out well.

CHAPTER 36
BABIES

Amira was returning from a hospital visit to Ide and her new baby. She sat in the corner of the Waldmeer cafe, thought about how adorable the baby was, and watched the Christmas holidaymakers. Her eyes were drawn to a mother and two girls at an outside table. The younger girl grabbed some of her sister's gingerbread man. A squabble ensued. Instead of dealing with it, the mother began to cry and rested her head in her hands. The youngest daughter looked worried and jumped up to pat her head. As the woman wiped her eyes, Amira realised it was Melissa, the mother of the girls she had looked after in Eraldus several years ago. On closer inspection, the fighting girls were indeed Marilyn and Bianca. They would now be eight and seven.

I see my darlings have returned to their naughty ways, thought Amira.

She probably meant Melissa as much as the children. Amira waited until the mother's tears had a chance to dry and then walked outside as if she hadn't seen them.

"Maria!" squealed both the children as Amira hugged them tightly.

Amira stopped working with the family before her Homeland transition and name change. They did not know that she lived in Waldmeer now. They all exchanged news, and the little family brightened up considerably. Melissa sent the girls across the road to the beach and spoke with Amira more earnestly.

"Much has happened in the last six months," said Melissa. "My husband and I have been through a rough patch. He became involved with an American woman who he was working with. He was honest enough to tell me about it, although we kept it from the children. We tried to work things out. We went to counselling, had many arguments, cried a lot, and then he left. He moved to the United States with his new partner, saying he would save money to bring the girls over for regular holidays. It's not just the emotional damage of the whole thing. The girls and I are having real survival issues. These days, my work means I am travelling all over the state. Obviously, that doesn't work with two little girls, and I have no relatives to help me. I have asked for work in the city, but they cannot give it to me for another year. I can't afford to lose this job. In desperation, I told the girls that we would have a few days in Waldmeer. I hoped that an angel would tell me what to do."

"I have an idea," said Amira suddenly. "Why don't I speak with Thomas MacArthur, the high school principal here in Waldmeer? He is a friend. I will ask him if the girls can enrol in the primary school for the year. Every Monday morning early, you could drive from Eraldus and drop them at school on your way to wherever you are going in the country. I will pick them up after school on Monday. They can stay with me for the school week and be picked up again by you after school on Friday."

"I don't know what to say," said Melissa. "I have to accept because I have no alternative. To say the girls will be thrilled is an understatement."

The girls ran wildly back from the beach. Bianca grabbed a piece of Marilyn's hair, and the older sister complained bitterly.

We'll be sorting out that behaviour fairly quickly, Amira thought.

"You tell the girls," said Amira. "I'll go and prepare my two spare bedrooms. Call in on your way home so that they can see where they will be staying."

Looks like I'll be getting my babies back, thought Amira.

CHAPTER 37
ANGEL

Although angels were not something Amira generally saw, there was one that she did occasionally see. She could *see* it just enough to know that it was large (larger than a person), took a masculine form, and (like all angels) was loving and powerful. However, she had not seen this angel for some time because she had not seen its accompanying human. It was Gabriel's angel. The angel only ever said one thing to Amira, which was repeated on several occasions. It was, *Be patient. He doesn't know what he is doing.* He would then look at Gabriel as if there was nothing he could do that could ever break that love. Amira never told Gabriel any of this because he didn't believe in angels, and he would have been offended that the angel thought that one needed patience to deal with him.

Amira hadn't seen Gabriel for the past six months. The six months before that, he occasionally came to Waldmeer and worked in the bungalow. One day, he told Amira that she should rent the bungalow out to someone else because he wasn't there enough. He said she should let him know when it had been arranged, and he would come and take all his things. Amira agreed, but she neither rented it out nor contacted him. He also did nothing, so the bungalow stood there with half-finished artwork and unused bed. The modest, little bungalow had been in the back garden a long time and, before that, had stood on the grounds of the Waldmeer hotel for even longer. It had time on its side.

CHAPTER 38
KAHWAH

Thomas was having one of his biannual styling visits with Gabriel. He would collect Gabriel once he got to Eraldus, drive to the large shopping centre, buy whatever Gabriel deemed worthy, have a coffee and a talk, and then go on to his other meetings in the city. Thomas's day would end with Kathleen over dinner. She always picked the restaurant. To get Thomas out of his comfort zone, she deliberately picked all sorts of weird and wonderful places.

Tonight, it was the *Afghan Light*. It was an endearing and interesting place. Everyone sat on elaborately decorated cushions inside a tent made from heavily embroidered fabrics, drinking tea called Kahwah. The tea was a combination of green tea, cardamom pods, cinnamon bark, saffron strands, ginger, and almonds. Like Masala tea from India and Kashmiri tea from Pakistan, the exact recipe is unique to each family. The first cup of tea was sweetened, and the next was not. Thomas mentioned to Kathleen that it was a bit like love.

"First," said Thomas, "you get pulled in by the loveliness, then you get beaten by the issues."

Kathleen laughed and replied, "Who would willingly walk the path of love without first being seduced by its promise?"

In his own way, Gabriel did a version of the restaurant choosing technique with Thomas's clothes. He would pick clothes for Thomas that were pushing the boundary but not over the line, hoping to modernise his style. He had mixed success. He could usually tell how the last six months had gone as soon as he saw whatever Thomas was wearing. Today, Thomas looked a little better. His pants were outdated, but his shirt was borderline okay. Quite frequently, Gabriel would pick things that looked great in the shop, but as soon as Thomas wore them, they seemed to change into looking different and less good. It was a work in progress.

"Did you know that Amira now has two little girls?" said Thomas over coffee.

"What?" said Gabriel.

"The little girls she looked after in Eraldus," said Thomas. "Their parents are separated. Amira has them at her house during the week, and the mother has them over the weekend in the family home they have always lived in. I believe it's not far from here."

"Yes, it's quite close,' said Gabriel, recalling where that family lived.

He sat there for a few minutes, trying to make sense of what Thomas had told him.

"How are things with Kathleen?" Gabriel asked, remembering that, on his last visit, Thomas had explained how happy and grateful he was that he and Kathleen had reconnected.

"It's been a year of seeing each other again," said Thomas. "It started slowly, but I probably see her most weeks now. She still won't come to Waldmeer, but I think we are making headway in rebuilding some trust."

"What do you think happened?" asked Gabriel, who was more interested in relationship failures and successes generally than Thomas's particular case.

Sensing this, Thomas said, "Have you not noticed that although we put enormous value on our couple relationships, they are minefields of hurt and betrayal, both real and imagined?"

Gabriel was listening. Thomas got into teaching mode. His teaching style had improved this year. It had a greater depth from hard-earned life experience and practising what he was preaching.

"Have you not noticed how much lying we do in them?" said Thomas honestly. "We tell ourselves it's not lies, or if it is, it is excusable for self-defence purposes. How little we realise that every lie digs us deeper into a painful delusion, and we end up building war zones, not love boats."

TOUCHED

CHAPTER 39
MISS YOU

Amira was admiring a different generation of sweet peas. This lot was winding up the footpath railing and onto the front doorsteps. They seemed to be singing a soft, repetitive song.

Tell him you miss him. Tell him you miss him.

After a while, Amira caught on and replied, "No, I won't."

Tell him you miss him.

"No, he's married."

Tell him you miss him.

"His partner will get upset with me if I tell him that."

Tell him you miss him.

"He doesn't care if I miss him or not."

Tell him you miss him.

Amira sighed and picked a couple of pretty sweet peas. It was pointless not to do as they wished—"they" being what was behind the sweet peas. She went inside, placed the flowers between two bits of paper, and put them in the middle of a heavy book.

A few days later, she took them out, and they had turned into pressed flowers. She carefully slid them into an envelope with a note saying, *I miss you.* She addressed the envelope to Gabriel, put it in the mailbox on the corner, and said to the wind, *I hope they know what they are talking about.*

CHAPTER 40
COURTING

Teresa and Bryan were going well. Well enough that, long ago, Teresa introduced Bryan to her girls. He only stayed overnight when the girls were with their father in the city, but he was a frequent day visitor when the girls were home. Teresa was conscious of protecting her girl's interests and not stressing them with a new family member. She was equally intent on keeping Bryan as her boyfriend. As he was relatively young and didn't have children, she felt he needed time to adjust to the demands of two girls in their early teens. She was realistic about step-parenting. It is hard enough for parents to come to terms with the unselfishness required for children, let alone step-parents who do not have the biological and emotional attachment to the child. Adjustment time on both sides and low expectations seemed the best approach. Teresa did her very best to make it all work.

Overall, it was working, with only minor problems now and again. However, after all her careful work, a bull had been let loose in the china shop. The girls had inadvertently let their father know about Bryan, and he was furious. Arthur was intelligent, vindictive, and unhappy—the right combination to create trouble in other people's lives. Further, he was an astute liar who always convinced himself that he was speaking the truth. He prided himself on his high ethics. Teresa did not take his trouble-making lightly. That would have been foolish. She did not tell Bryan anything about it as she didn't want to burden him. Anyway, she felt Arthur was a problem she had invited into her own life, so it was up to her to deal with him. Although she was correct about Arthur, she underestimated Bryan.

A solicitor's letter arrived saying that Arthur would fight for sole custody of the girls because their mother was providing "an unsuitable and unstable environment due to her young male companions." He said that he was better equipped to raise them. Teresa knew that Arthur did not really want the girls—he was far too busy, and they would end up on their own for long periods— but he would employ the best lawyers. He was a convincing actor and would present well in court. Teresa worried that, in comparison, she might come across as less than marvellous. Besides, no matter how she came across, she knew the impact a powerful, wealthy, and determined man could have in any situation.

Teresa was angry, but more than that, she was scared. This would have an enormous effect on her girl's well-being. She tried to reassure herself that although Arthur had the fire of vindictiveness, she had the fire of a mother's love.

CHAPTER 41
GIRL-BED

The girls and Amira sat at the round kitchen table, having dinner. The dusk had receded, and it was getting dark, but Amira hadn't bothered to close the curtains. In Waldmeer, it didn't matter.

Two headlights appeared not far from the window. They all wondered who it was. The girls ran outside, eager for any visitor. However, when they saw it was a man they didn't know, they quickly ran back inside.

It was Gabriel.

After Amira waved to him, the girls deemed it safe and decided to follow him down to the bungalow. He didn't send them away. With the openness of children, they would stay with him for as long as he allowed.

About fifteen minutes later, the three of them appeared at the back door of the main house.

"There's water all over the bungalow," said Marilyn, anxious to report the news.

"Oh no," said Amira. "Is there a leak?"

"Yes," said Gabriel. "It's above the bed. My art stuff is fine, but the bed is wet."

They all went to investigate, and Amira brought a bucket. There was no room to move the bed, so Gabriel lifted it onto its side. He guessed where the leak was coming from and put the bucket there.

"I'll fix it later," he said.

Amira was not as confident in Gabriel's handyman skills as he was, but said, "Sure," not wanting to dampen his enthusiasm.

"I told Gabriel that he can have my room tonight, and I'll sleep in with Marilyn," said Bianca, wanting to keep their visitor longer.

The girls missed their Dad. Amira looked at Gabriel, who wasn't objecting.

"If he doesn't mind sleeping in a girl-bed," she said.

Gabriel smiled at Amira and said, "I have done that before."

And that was the first of Gabriel's staying in the girl-bed, which happened numerous times over the coming months. He kept saying he would fix the roof, but needed to find out how. He didn't seem in any great hurry.

ON ONE OF Gabriel's visits, Amira asked him about Paul.

"We separated six months ago," said Gabriel.

Amira was surprised that he hadn't already told her.

"I didn't want to be part of the divorce statistic," said Gabriel, "but now I am. Because we were married less than two years, we had to go to a counselling session."

"How was that?" asked Amira.

"Terrible. Painful."

Gabriel looked disgusted with the whole thing and said, "Never again."

Amira wasn't sure if he meant never again for marriage or never again for divorce, but assumed both by the look on Gabriel's face.

"How is Paul?" she asked, feeling that Paul would be suffering more from the whole process.

"He'll be fine," said Gabriel. "He'll find someone else."

CHAPTER 42
TOY BOY

"What the hell?" said Bryan.

Teresa had never seen him even close to this angry.

"You thought you would keep the whole thing about Arthur and the court case to yourself? Why, in God's name, would you do that? Do you think I am incapable—a child?"

He added sarcastically, "In case you haven't noticed, I'm a grown man."

"Of course, you are," said Teresa, "but...."

"Don't you trust me? Do you respect me so little? What else haven't you told me?" he demanded. "What else?"

"You're being silly," said Teresa quietly.

Bryan was in no mood for correction.

"I thought we were in this together," he said. "Obviously, not. Am I some sort of toy boy that's good for fun but not much else?"

Toy boy was a word Teresa never said around Bryan because she thought it was insulting to both.

"Am I just a rebound from Arthur," said Bryan, "to amuse you for a while when your girls aren't around?"

Holding her face in his hands, he said, "You have no intention of having a serious relationship with me, do you?"

He grabbed his jacket and slammed the door.

Neither Teresa nor Bryan slept much that night. The girls were in the city with their father, so Teresa's flat was particularly empty. It was above the Waldmeer bookshop and overlooked the main beach. She opened the balcony door at 4.00 a.m. The breeze off the water was fresh. The sky was a mixture of clouds, stars, and a half-formed moon, which sporadically appeared between the clouds as if to remind anyone watching that it may be hidden but was not absent. Although Teresa was very upset about the argument and worried it might be their last one, she could not help feeling a little pleased that Bryan cared about being in her life that much. On that partially comforting note, she went back to bed to get an hour or two of sleep.

She didn't contact Bryan over the coming days because she felt that if he was going to return, he had to do so when he was ready. It only took two days. Bryan was a straightforward person. He didn't dwell on things. He said what he wanted, and troubles would fade from his mind without consciously trying. This trouble didn't exactly *fade from his mind,* but the anger did and was replaced with an idea. When Teresa opened the door and saw it was Bryan, tears came to her eyes. She wasn't one to cry in front of people. She spent too long in a fragmented marriage to do that. Bryan hugged her, and they only reluctantly let go of each other. They sat on the balcony together, drinking herbal tea.

"I have an idea," said Bryan. "I think we should get engaged."

Teresa spat out her tea. Bryan knew she would be unprepared, so he didn't take offence. He even laughed.

When Teresa realised he was serious, she took his hand and said softly, "Bryan, I love you. It's that simple. But you haven't had your children yet, and I wouldn't take that away from you."

Teresa may not have been prepared for this discussion, but Bryan was.

"I think," he said, "we have already discussed the point of my being quite capable of making my own decisions."

"Yes, we have," said Teresa, smiling.

"It might help with the court case for you to have a stable relationship," said Bryan.

"And you may feel more willing to share the girls with me," he added hopefully. "Regardless, I want to marry you."

He looked towards the ocean. It was so familiar to him.

"You have had a far more interesting life than I," he continued. "I have only ever lived here. But I don't need to live anywhere else to know what I want. I don't think you are ready to marry me at this stage, but if we get engaged, I don't care how long it takes you to get there."

Teresa was truly stunned by Bryan's maturity. She felt embarrassed to have not seen it before, but told herself that maybe it wasn't there before.

It is there now, she thought. *Right now, he is more of a teacher than any kind of a "toy". I guess that's what love does. Those we love become our teachers, whether we intend it or not.*

HOPE

CHAPTER 43
OPPORTUNITY

Teresa had eight big bags lined up. They were full of her rich clothes from the years with Arthur. Two by two, she took the bags down the stairs, past her bookshop, to the Op Shop a few doors away.

When the shop assistant started unpacking them and saw the expensive brand names, she said kindly, "Are you sure you want to give us all these beautiful clothes, dear? They've hardly been worn."

The manager, who was in the Country Women's Association with Teresa's mother, entered from the backroom and said, "I see you are having a big clean-up. *A clean-up is as good as a holiday.*"

Teresa smiled at her misquoting the saying that *a change is as good as a holiday,* but thought that a clean-up was as good as a change, and both were as good as a holiday.

"THAT'S the daughter of the Hemingways," said the shop manager to the assistant when they were both in the back room. "She left Waldmeer years ago to marry an older man —a tycoon. It didn't work out, and now she's back in Waldmeer with her daughters."

"Oh, is that who she is?" said the other woman.

"I heard she is now engaged to Bryan, Clarice's youngest child," said the shop manager. "They are the farm next to the Hemingways. Teresa would have known him when he was a child."

"She's gone from gold digger to cougar," said the other woman.

"Amelia!" the shop manager scolded, but also smiled in good-natured amusement.

"Don't you worry," said Amelia mischievously. "Who wants money when you can have fun?"

The shop manager slapped her wrist and said, "Well, keep away from my sons. And half your luck if you find someone else."

CHAPTER 44
REBORN

Teresa's eldest daughter, Josephine, and Ide's eldest son, Christopher, were both fourteen and in the same year level at Waldmeer State Secondary School. The two mothers usually sat together at school meetings and functions. Their mutual connection to Amira cemented their friendship, but it had its own flavour.

When the three women were together or when Amira was with either of them separately, conversations took the path that Amira designated. Amira didn't mind the topic, but she did mind the direction of any conversation. If either of the women had a problem and wanted to discuss it, Amira was more than happy to let them express their feelings. However, she would not allow conversations to deteriorate into complaining, blaming, gossiping or laughing at other people's expense. When it came to the general public, Amira would quickly exit destructive or pointless conversations. However, if her *trusted ones* were the conversationalists, she would correct them and then exit the conversation.

Ide and Teresa were both very aware of this and some-times laughed to each other that they just needed to have a good old bitch.

"Don't go to Amira if you want to bitch," they would say to each other. "You'll get a lecture."

They only ever trusted each other with Amira-jokes because they knew their loyalty to her was unquestioned. Away from Amira and within the safety of their friendship, they sometimes took the opportunity to bitch, laugh, and complain about life as much as they wanted. Not only would it not be repeated, but most of the time, it was not even taken seriously. Teresa's favourite topic of complaint was Arthur. Ide oscillated between the hospital matron and Farkas, although she loved the latter and not the former.

Lately, whenever Ide, Teresa, and their children were together, Christopher took his baby brother off Ide's lap, carried him over to Josephine, and presented her with the baby. Josephine was always thrilled, and they would play with the baby for as long as the circumstances would allow. Christopher was not an average type of fourteen-year-old boy, although he was well-liked by his peers. He was a creative soul and a searching thinker. He was more inter-ested in people than in any of the things that his male peers were interested in. While his peers treated girls as some sort of annoying but captivating entity to somehow be organised into submission, Christopher saw them as people—interest-ing, intelligent, and of value to his being.

"Have you noticed how close Christopher and Josephine are becoming?" Ide said to Teresa.

"Yes, I have," said Teresa.

Both women watched the two young friends playing with the baby.

"Love never fails to save the world," said Teresa.

"It keeps getting reborn," said Ide.

"Love or the world?" asked Teresa.

"Both," replied Ide.

CHAPTER 45
THE LIST

"I was going to ring you," said Teresa as Amira entered the bookshop. "I have the most wonderful news."

"Yes, I know," said Amira, smiling. "You're engaged. You already told me."

Teresa rolled her eyes.

"No, seriously, I have big news about your manuscript. Someone from Hope Publishing in the States rang this morning and is interested in it."

"Really?" said Amira in surprise.

Last year, once her house in Eraldus was sold, Amira started to write newsletters for her clients in the city. She didn't have the girls to attend to as she did now, and the number of clients she saw in Waldmeer was relatively few. Waldmeer was, after all, a small, coastal village. Healers were hardly the first port of call for most of its residents.

As she had time on her hands, Amira spent it in her garden or writing the letters. They became longer and more frequent. By the end of the year, she had enough of them to edit together into a book. She printed, bound, and sent it to her city clients as a present. Teresa was listed as author-agent. She wasn't an agent, but she *was* willing and a bookshop owner.

At the time, Amira told Teresa, "We will both be in this together. It will be the blind leading the blind or, more fortuitously, companion adventurers."

"One of your city clients gave the manuscript to her brother, who was visiting from the States," said Teresa. "He loved it and gave it to his friend at Hope Publishing. They are one of the biggest self-help publishers. They said they want you to travel to Los Angeles and sign a book contract if all goes well. You would need to live there some of the year to promote the book and future ones."

Teresa stared wide-eyed at Amira and said, "This is every author's dream. If they publish you, you could end up on the New York Times Best Seller list."

Amira was silent.

"Here is their number," continued Teresa. "Ring them today."

As Amira turned for the door, still having said nothing, Teresa added, "One more thing. His last words to me were, 'We need a new guru. Several of our bestselling ones have died. I think your author may fit the bill. She's strange enough to be interesting, sincere enough to be believed, and lives in an exotic enough location to fascinate our U.S. readership. She's sellable, and our job is selling. We believe we have a match.'"

Still trying to get some response from Amira, Teresa said, "This is an offer you can't refuse."

"No, I suppose not," said Amira.

Once Amira had closed the shop door, Teresa thought, *They sure got the "strange" bit right.*

PEACE

CHAPTER 46
REUNION

"Why are you here, Amira?" asked Thomas. "This is not your year level."

It was the ten-year reunion of Maria-Amira's graduating class. Everyone was now twenty-eight. The problem was that although Maria would have been twenty-eight, Amira had gained twelve years in terms of biology and demeanour during her Homeland transition more than two years ago. That made her forty, around the same age as Gabriel and Charlie. It's not that she looked forty. She had a relatively ageless appearance. However, her demeanour was certainly not that of a younger adult. She was told in the Homeland that those who had previously known her would gradually forget how old she was supposed to be and relate to her as she was now. That is exactly what happened. Understandably, Amira was reluctant to go to the reunion and remind everyone of her birth age, but as she lived in Waldmeer, she had no viable excuse not to go.

"This is my correct year level," said Amira.

Thomas looked confused, but then told himself that he had been there so long that it all rolled into one, and he didn't think about it again.

One of those attending was Mary, Charlie's partner of the last five years. Charlie didn't come. Mary took the opportunity to visit her parents, Grace and Joe. Mary's twin brother, Harry, was also there. Harry had been a bully at school and afterwards. Charlie had been the brunt of his and his mates' jokes for many years.

"Wow, a blast from the past," Harry said to Amira. "I haven't seen you for ages. I must tell you that I had a crush on you once you sorted me out about bullying Charlie."

Amira smiled and recalled how he would occasionally send anonymous flowers to her mother's cafe for her. She would recognise his handwriting from school.

"What are you doing these days?" asked Amira.

"I went to university and did teaching," said Harry. "I work in the city at one of the state secondary schools."

"It's a rough area, but they say I'm okay with the kids," he said in an understated, country-boy way.

Amira surmised that he would be terrific with the kids, having just the right combination of toughness, no-nonsense authority, and understanding wrought from personal experience.

"That's wonderful. Congratulations," said Amira.

They both knew she meant, *Congratulations on coming such a long way from the bullying idiot you once were.*

Harry then looked at Amira intently.

"It's peculiar," he said. "You always seemed so young and innocent, but now I look at you, and you seem more like my mother."

Amira laughed and said, "Thanks, Harry. You look great, too."

CHAPTER 47
DEAR DAD

Teresa's girls had not long left for school. She usually waved them off from the balcony, and then they had an idyllic walk along the sea path and up the hill. The fresh ocean air could sweep away a substantial part of a schoolgirl's cares before the day even started.

Before opening the shop, Teresa attended to some housework. As she vacuumed Josephine's floor, she noticed a pile of paper in the waste paper bin. It looked like many drafts of something. She could see that one of the papers on the top was a letter addressed to Josephine's father. Not one to overstep the boundaries of a teenage girl, Teresa nevertheless looked more closely at the letter. Due to the escalating court troubles she was having with Arthur, she wanted to ensure he was not manipulating the girls with false information or intimidation. In this particular case, he wasn't. It was Josephine who initiated the letter. Teresa sat down and read the draft.

Dear Dad,

I hope you don't mind me writing to you. I have a friend (not a boyfriend, Dad) named Christopher. Last weekend, I went with him to see some of his relatives in the back hills of Waldmeer. The relatives are called Clinkers. They are a bit like gypsies. Don't worry. They aren't going to steal me. Christopher told me that the main guy, who runs the ceremonies, is magic. He can see things. I'm not sure what. Christopher doesn't know, either. After the ceremony, I asked the magic man if he could see anything in me. I thought he would say no, but he didn't. He said, "One day, you will be influential in the financial world. You must pay attention to your studies as you will need them. You must remember to be brave and live by your highest beliefs, as that will give you success. You chose your mother and father because you need your mother's emotional intelligence and your father's business acumen to fulfil your function. Also, you will learn from your father's mistakes." Sorry about that last bit. I haven't told Mum, but I thought I would tell you because it would be nice if we could all be friends, seeing as I picked you both.

Love from your daughter, Josephine.

Teresa sat on the bed, holding the draft. She was shaken for numerous reasons. Finance was probably the last field she wanted her daughter to enter after her experience with Arthur. However, more than that, she suddenly felt that the fighting was irrelevant to what mattered. With all Arthur's faults, he still had good qualities. Otherwise, why would she ever have married him? And regardless, Josephine had apparently chosen him for good and bad. It was, indeed, sobering.

She never mentioned the letter to Josephine, and Josephine never mentioned it to her. Teresa was unsure if she ever mailed a final version to her father. However, Teresa's attitude to Arthur had significantly softened. She no longer felt the anger that had been welling up inside her for months. It had disintegrated. Replacing it was a sense that everything could work out without anyone being hurt. For whatever reason, Teresa never received another letter from Arthur's lawyers. No one ever spoke about the court case or getting sole custody again. The whole thing vanished into thin air as if it had never even existed.

CHAPTER 48
CUDDLE

The following weekend, Teresa walked with Bryan at the beach and tried to explain how her feelings towards Arthur had changed. She couldn't mention the letter because that was an issue of Josephine's privacy. However, as Bryan had made it clear that he wanted her to share her life, she tried to talk about what had happened. Bryan could tell that the anger towards Arthur had been replaced with understanding and perhaps even some affection. He said all the right things, but the conversation remained with him uneasily. He started to worry that Teresa might reconnect with Arthur. Although he knew it was unlikely, he couldn't stop the stream of thought.

I can't compete with him, thought Bryan. *He's used to winning.*

Over the next few weeks, Bryan started to withdraw from Teresa. Usually, he slept at her flat and then travelled to the family farm early each morning. However, he was increasingly staying at the farm overnight. He told her that the days there were so long at the moment that he needed to be there at the crack of dawn. Teresa felt him pulling away, but couldn't do anything about it. It scared her. It scared her differently from what Arthur's court case had done. Arthur scared her into protecting her children. This was scaring her deep within her being.

Of course, Clarice was delighted to have her son back. She would make little comments like, "You always have your room here if things don't quite go to plan. Sometimes things happen for a reason."

Bryan would get angry with her and walk outside.

One morning before opening the bookshop, Teresa called into the Op Shop. She could see that her rich clothes were fast disappearing.

"We have lots of happy customers who love the clothes you brought in," said the shop manager.

"That's terrific," said Teresa. "I'm glad they are feeling loved."

Sensing that Teresa looked a little glum, the shop manager said, "How's that young man of yours?"

Teresa responded to her motherliness, saying, "Actually, not that good. He's back home a lot. I think he doesn't trust me."

"Of course he does, dear," said the shop manager, "but, you know, when we put our heart into a relationship, we are very vulnerable. We make up things because the other person has so much power to hurt us. Be patient and let him know that you love him. He'll sort it out himself."

The shop manager saw Clarice at the Country Women's Association monthly meeting that evening. She knew that Clarice would be elated at having her precious Bryan back home.

After the meeting, she handed Clarice some cake and

said as if it had only just entered her mind, "We have been fortunate with our marriages, haven't we? They require a lot of give and take over the years, but we both still have our marriages, and they are very respectable, if I do say so myself. We can only hope that our children have the same good fortune."

Clarice ate her cake in silence.

The next afternoon, Bryan called into the bookshop just before closing.

"I'll make dinner tonight," he said.

Trying not to look surprised, Teresa said, "Great."

"And then we can have an early night," said Bryan.

He must be staying the night, thought Teresa.

"That sounds lovely," she said.

"Maybe, even have a bit of a cuddle," said Bryan, smiling.

Teresa then knew he was back. She didn't know why he was back. She didn't care why. She was simply relieved.

That night, after their *bit of a cuddle*, Bryan turned out the bedside lamp and said in the dark, "This morning, my mother said something very peculiar to me."

"What did she say?" asked Teresa.

"She said that although she loved having me home," said Bryan, "you probably missed me and that as she wasn't the number one woman in my life anymore, I should be getting back to you before you run off with someone else."

Teresa was more stunned than Bryan had been.

Bryan pulled her to him and said, "I don't want you to run off with someone else, but if you ever did, it would have still been all worth it. I would not regret a single instant."

He rolled over and fell into a peaceful sleep. So did Teresa.

FAME

CHAPTER 49
WORDS

G abriel had started dating again, male and female. He didn't sleep with any of them. These days, he was too old to imagine that one could sleep with another person without paying the price. He wasn't willing to pay that price, so he didn't.

Amira told him about her upcoming trip to Los Angeles. It would soon be the school holidays. She was going to take Marilyn and Bianca to the States so they could see their father.

"My Eraldus lease is coming up for renewal," said Gabriel when next he was in Waldmeer.

Since Paul moved out, there was only Gabriel in the house.

"The house is too expensive for me," he continued, "but I don't have any clear idea of where to go next."

"The girls and I will be gone by next weekend," said Amira, "and we'll be away for a month. Why don't you stay here for the month?"

With no better alternative, Gabriel agreed.

Besides briefly telling him about her trip, Amira hadn't mentioned much else because he didn't want to discuss it. She left her manuscript on the lounge room table so he could look at it if he wanted.

"Have you had a look at my book?" asked Amira.

"I hate reading. You know that," said Gabriel.

He tried reading the first chapter but didn't even reach the bottom of the first page. Another time, he tried another chapter. He didn't do much better. He read it at night when everyone was asleep. He was a night person. Amira was a morning person.

"I looked at it," said Gabriel one morning, not explaining what he had looked at.

Amira knew what it was.

"And? Do you like it?" she asked.

"No. I don't understand it," said Gabriel. "The words are too big."

He said it as if it were the fault of the words that were being difficult to get along with.

"And the ideas are too complicated," he complained.

Gabriel spoke dismissively because he didn't like Amira's new life direction, though there was some truth in what he said.

CHAPTER 50
ON THE LINE

A few weeks passed with Gabriel living in Waldmeer. This morning, he stood behind Farkas at the baker's. They nodded to each other as men do. Ide and the baby had softened Farkas. He was more settled, although *settled* and *Farkas* didn't quite go together.

"You at Amira's while she is in the States?" asked Farkas.

"Yep," said Gabriel.

"What do you think about Amira's book contract?" he added after a pause.

Farkas looked surprised that his opinion was being sought and answered, "She was always going to do well."

"Yeah?" said Gabriel.

"I have known her for a long time," said Farkas.

"How long?" asked Gabriel, realising he had no idea how Farkas and Amira first met.

Farkas paused and said, "Longer than I can remember."

"I remember you knew her already when I first met her at Waldmeer Corner Store and Cafe," said Gabriel.

"Back then, she was just a girl," said Farkas. "Not anymore."

Farkas smiled and continued, "You have to be brave to take her on now. I'm brave. Not that brave."

"I don't think so," said Gabriel.

"Don't think what?" said Farkas. "That I'm not that brave or that she is trouble?"

Gabriel didn't reply. He didn't want to enter either of those conversations.

Farkas's face relaxed.

"She is not the sort of person that can be controlled," he said.

Gabriel shrugged as if it were of no relevance to him.

"She doesn't even control herself," said Farkas.

Gabriel glanced towards the counter to see how far the line had progressed, and said, "Oh my God, this line is ridiculous. It hasn't even moved."

He left.

There was only one person in front of Farkas.

CHAPTER 51
UNNECESSARY

n the US:

A few days before Amira was due to return home from the States, she received a phone call from Marilyn and Bianca's father, Peter. Amira thought he would be ringing to confirm where he would meet her at the airport so she could collect the girls.

"Hi, Pete. How are you?" said Amira.

"We're all good, thanks," said Peter brightly.

Amira surmised that his time with the girls must have gone well.

"I'm glad," she said.

"I'm ringing to let you know I will be returning home on the same flight as you," said Peter.

Home? thought Amira. *I thought here was home now.*

"I might as well tell you," said Peter, "because it will affect your life as well as ours. I'm going to try to work things out with Melissa."

"Okay," said Amira. "I hope it does work out."

In Eraldus:

Peter and Melissa were sitting at an outside table at the Eraldus cafe.

"It feels good to be back," said Peter. "Thanks for coming to talk with me. How are the girls after their long flight?"

"Exhausted," said Melissa. "They are still asleep."

She looked at Peter, who was fidgeting in an uncustomary fashion. He had always held most of the cards in their marriage.

"They said they had a lovely time with you," said Melissa.

Peter smiled and lightened a little.

"I forgot about the incomprehensible and unpredictable weather here," he said, pulling up his collar. "Why, on earth, is it cold at this time of the year?"

"Well, you didn't dress appropriately," scolded Melissa in a good-natured way.

"Nonsense!" said Peter. "It's the damn weather that is inappropriate, not me."

Melissa laughed and was happy to hear one of his old jokes. Somehow, it seemed funny again. Nothing he had said for the last year seemed even remotely funny.

After their breakfast and a chat about incidental things, Melissa stood up. Peter watched her. He had not mentioned anything about his plan to return.

"Well, I think the girls will be awake by now," said Melissa. "They have become so used to seeing you every day that you'd better walk home with me so they can talk to you."

After paying, they headed for home. Peter brushed a

finger against Melissa's hand. He was terrified that she would pull away. It was one of the most important and frightening moments of his life.

She put her hand in his and said nothing. In fact, nothing was ever said about Peter's time in the States or his return to Melissa.

It was not necessary.

CHAPTER 52
STORY

I*n Waldmeer:*

Although Gabriel enjoyed having the house to himself, he missed Amira. He missed her more because he didn't know how much she would even be in Waldmeer in the future. He got a lot of work done without the distractions of the city. He was pleased with that, less pleased with himself. Reluctant to admit it, he was affected by his conversation with Farkas.

Everything seems fine, thought Gabriel, *and then things start unravelling on their own for no rational reason.*

He decided to be more honest. After all, no one could hear him but himself.

Who am I kidding? I push Amira away, myself. It's easy to be nice to people who don't mean that much to us. But if something matters to us, we will fight to make it work in our favour. Do we even know what is in our favour?

He walked outside and listened to the faint sounds of the sea at the bottom of the hill. He watched the kookaburras eyeing him off. Yesterday, one of them swooped down and grabbed a whole sandwich out of his hand. Their beaks are strong.

"You won't get me again, you thief," yelled Gabriel. "You missed my face by one centimetre!"

"I HAVE SOMETHING FOR YOU," said Amira the following evening.

She quickly unpacked and took a pile of papers, clipped together, from her bag.

"Another book," groaned Gabriel. "I don't want it. I didn't even like the first one."

"It's not a book," said Amira, undeterred by Gabriel's off-hand manner. "It's only two chapters."

She left it on the kitchen bench, knowing that if he were going to read it, it would be late at night.

THE NEXT DAY, Amira said, "You haven't asked me about my trip or the children. Haven't you noticed they are not here?"

"Yes, of course, I noticed," said Gabriel. "I assumed they were still in the city."

"Peter and Melissa are most likely reuniting," said Amira, "and the children will return to their old Eraldus school. They won't be here anymore."

Gabriel looked at Amira. She seemed somewhat sad. She probably liked having the girls because she didn't have her own children.

"Oh, I'm sorry," he said. "But it's for the best. They need to be with their parents."

"Yes," said Amira, who always knew their stay was temporary.

"You still have me," said Gabriel.

Amira smiled and said, "Bianca doesn't need her room anymore, so you are welcome to it for as long as you want."

"I'm returning to Eraldus this afternoon to deal with some work," said Gabriel. "I'll stay with a friend. I'll be back in a few days."

When he was leaving, he said, "Your new book is a story. I read it last night."

"Yes, it is. Did you understand it better than my other book?" asked Amira.

"Yes, I did," said Gabriel.

"And?" asked Amira.

"It made me think, but at least I knew what I was supposed to be thinking about," said Gabriel.

"And?" asked Amira again.

"I've had a whole month of thinking," said Gabriel. "Way too much thinking for me."

He hugged her goodbye and said, "See you in two days."

CHAPTER 53
UNRECOGNISABLE

In the Leleks:

The forest was shining with soft, wavering light. It was a pristine, sacred morning.

Perfect, thought Amira.

Although she had seen Erdo a few times in town during the last two years, she had not driven out to see him in the Leleks since before her Eraldus days. Erdo was waiting on the other side of the old walking bridge. Amira saw two splendid black swans on the lake and wondered if it was the same pair she had often seen years ago.

"Yes, it is," said Erdo. "Swans mate for life, although sometimes they part if nesting fails. Otherwise, they work with the bond they've made."

Amira sat on a decaying tree trunk and watched the lake, which always seemed to have a special enchantment.

After about ten minutes, she said, "I haven't told anyone yet, but I didn't sign the book contract."

Erdo nodded.

"The first two weeks in the States were a whirlwind of

meetings, interviews, bookstores, lawyers, and experts," said Amira.

One of the swans suddenly departed, but the mate stayed. Amira waited to see what would happen next. Nothing happened, so she continued.

"I hated it," she said. "I hated every minute of it."

"Is that why you didn't sign?" asked Erdo.

"I started to dream of Alamgir," said Amira. "I kept expecting to see him, but I never did. I'd know that dark malevolence anywhere. I was a little anxious that I might see him here today as I did one other time."

Erdo put his hands in the air and pointed at the tranquil surroundings to indicate he was not there.

"They organised a whole month of engagements for me," explained Amira, "but I'd made my decision before two weeks were up. I told them that I wasn't their guru. They were rather stunned and tried to talk me out of it. When they couldn't, they aborted mission and returned my manuscript. That was the last I heard of them. After that, I spent a few days wandering—beaches, parks, streets. I tried not to think about anything in particular."

The swan returned, and its mate swam over and circled it with effortless fluidity. It was all grace and poise.

"And then," said Amira, "I started to write something new, something different—a story. So, I knew it was the right decision."

"I'm an old hermit who lives away from the world. I know nothing of publishing," said Erdo.

"Yes, but you have sources," said Amira. "Inside information."

"It was the right decision," said Erdo. "The seduction of success and fame is great and treacherous."

He wandered over to the lake and threw a stick into the middle of the water. He watched as the rings spread to the edge.

"And what of Alamgir?" asked Amira. "I still haven't seen him, and he always comes to me if I start dreaming of him."

"Oh, you saw him," said Erdo. "You saw him many times when you were away. You just didn't recognise him."

CHAPTER 54
FURTHER

"I'm sorry that it didn't work out how you wanted," said Amira to Teresa. "It might be every author's dream, but I don't dream about such things."

"Do it your way," said Teresa in a resigned manner. "However, I do wish we had something we could give people. Right now, we have nothing."

"We have hope," said Amira. "A hope that will not delude or deceive and will include everyone and disadvantage no one."

Teresa nodded.

"I may not have dreams of fame," said Amira, "but I dream for the world."

Teresa ran her hand along one of the shelves as if trying to make something more concrete materialise in her safe, little corner of the world.

Amira touched her hand and said, "And we have these."

She pulled five books out of her bag. In her last two weeks in the States, Amira had her manuscript made into some paperbacks without the help of the publishers.

Given something more tangible, Teresa's expression gladdened. She took the books and created a space on the shelf.

Looking up at Amira hopefully, she said, "We have all come this far together. Together, we can go further."

SUMMARY OF WALDMEER SERIES

A multi-generational journey of spiritual awakening, healing, and the spaces between worlds.

Beneath the surface of an idyllic coastal village, unseen forces stir. Waldmeer is a place where the visible and invisible meet—where inter-dimensional realms brush against everyday life, and where emotional truths rise quietly but undeniably.

Told across seven books, the *Waldmeer Series* follows Maria–Amira from the groundedness of her rural home to the doorways into higher realms of perception and spiritual transformation. Around her, those she loves and seeks to help are drawn into their own awakenings, resistances, and reckonings.

Waldmeer moves between ordinary moments and otherworldly initiations. Between earthly love and higher love. Between who we think we are... and what we truly are.

At times tender, at times confronting, these stories unfold in layers—personal, relational, and metaphysical.

ABOUT THE AUTHOR

*On the beach at Lorne,
Australia (the coastal village
Waldmeer is based on).*

Donna Goddard is a spiritual author whose work blends clarity, devotion, and metaphysical insight. With more than twenty published books across spiritual nonfiction, fiction, poetry, and children's literature, she writes to uplift consciousness and offer healing through words.

Donna's Facebook author page has over 400,000 followers worldwide, and her YouTube channel has received 4 million views. Her books are read by spiritual seekers globally and are known for their honesty, poetic style, and transformative energy.

Her writing is an offering—to help others awaken their own inner spirit, trust its guidance, and create a life of depth, beauty, and quiet joy.

All links at https://linktr.ee/donnagoddard

Ratings and Reviews

Donna would be grateful for any ratings or reviews.

ALSO BY DONNA GODDARD

Fiction

Waldmeer Series: A Spiritual Fiction Series
Nanima Series: Spiritual Fiction
Enanika Series: Visionary Fiction
Riverland Series (children's fiction 6 to 9 years)
Foxie (children's fiction 7 to 12 years)

Nonfiction

Love and Devotion Series
Sweet Spirit Series
Consciousness Series
Meditation Series
Poetry Series
Love's Longing
Dance: A Spiritual Affair
Writing: A Spiritual Voice

www.ingramcontent.com/pod-product-compliance
Lightning Source LLC
Chambersburg PA
CBHW020517120726
47904CB00003B/869